. . . .
SHADOW OF THE WOLF

SHADOW OF THE WOLF

. . . .

An Apache Tale

By Harry James Plumlee

UNIVERSITY OF OKLAHOMA PRESS
Norman and London

This is a work of fiction. Although some of the names, characters, places, and incidents are based on historical fact, their depiction is a product of the author's imagination.

Library of Congress Cataloging-in-Publication Data

Plumlee, Harry James, 1944–
    Shadow of the wolf: an Apache tale / by Harry James Plumlee.
      p. cm.
    ISBN: 0–8061–2905–0 (alk. paper)
    1. Indians of North America—Arizona—Wars—Fiction.
    2. Apache Indians—Wars—Fiction.   I. Title.
    PS3566.L76S563   1997
    813'.54—dc20   96–34556
                                               CIP

Text design by Cathy Carney Imboden.
Text is set in Baskerville.

The paper in this book meets the guidelines for permanence and durability of the Committee on Production Guidelines for Book Longevity of the Council on Library Resources, Inc. ∞

1 2 3 4 5 6 7 8 9 10

. . . .

In loving memory of my mother,
Clara Plumlee

ACKNOWLEDGMENTS

I am grateful to all of those who offered encouragement, suggestions on my manuscript, or editorial assistance. They include Tom Bone, Pam Bone, Travis Bone, Danielle Terrasi, and my wife, Valerie Ann Plumlee.

Chapter epigraphs consisting of previously published copyrighted material are used by permission of the publishers. The epigraphs for chapters 2, 4, and 23 are from *Western Apache Raiding and Warfare: From the Notes of Grenville Goodwin,* edited by Keith H. Basso, copyright University of Arizona press, 1971; the epigraphs for chapters 5, 15, and 26 are from *Apache Days and After,* by Thomas Cruse, copyright Caxton Printers, 1941; the epigraph for chapter 6 is from *With the Scouts and Cavalry at Fort Apache,* by Col. H. B. Wharfield, copyright Arizona Historical Society, 1965; the epigraph for chapter 18 is from *John Spring's Arizona,* edited by A. M. Gustafson, copyright University of Arizona Press, 1966.

SHADOW OF THE WOLF

Apacheria, circa 1870

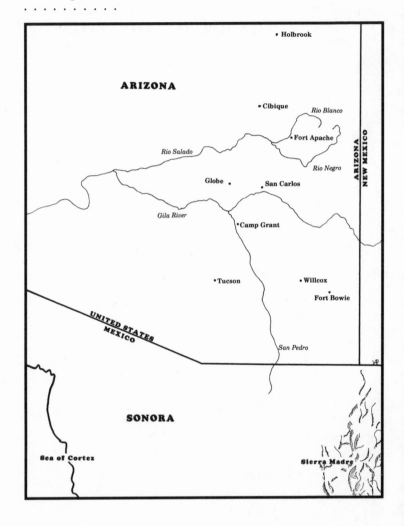

The Apache had few wants and cared for no luxuries. War was his business, his life, and victory his dream. To attack a Mexican camp or isolated village, he would gladly travel hundreds of miles, incurring every risk.

John G. Bourke,
General Crook in the Indian Country

"It is good to kill Mexicans," considered Nakaidoklinni as he signaled to Sanchez to keep the horses quiet. The trap was nearly sprung, and once more parting the grama grass, he spied, with steadfast anticipation in his heart, on the dusty track below. A *conducta*. This was his third raid to Mexico and always before they had taken horses, cattle, or burros from isolated ranchos, happy to be given meat to take back to the *gota*. But now, a small *conducta* was wending its way, one hoofed step at a time, to the narrow passage where the white rocks constricted the canyon far below the crest of the hill.

One, two, three burros reappeared from the obscuring mesquite, then three more, pushed by two Mexicans on horses, each leading a mule. Now the faint tink of the bell could be heard from the lead burro urging the others onward to the white rocks. Nakaidoklinni offered prayer using the special words of war language that he and Sanchez had learned. He prayed that the power of the warriors would be strong, and that killing the Mexicans would be like killing a deer or even a rabbit; but he was careful to ask this in a humble way because boastful pride or too much confidence must be guarded against when on a raid.

The lead burro raised its shaggy gray head and picked up the pace, scenting the water flowing from the spring in the rocks. Its pack jounced unevenly in response to the jerky gait. There was something strange on the last Mexican, thought Nakaidoklinni. He saw a brown belt around his waist, and as he wondered what it might be, it disappeared behind the man and then moved again into view. So! He has a child with him. How old, he wondered. Is it a boy or a girl? It shouldn't be long until he would have the answer to his question. The last burro had splashed into the sandy basin at the foot of the rocks and was drinking thirstily from the cool, clear waters.

Nakaidoklinni was tense and utterly still. Only his eyes moved as he searched for any movement, any sign from below that the Mexican *conducta* was about to belong to the raiding Apaches. The last horse had now appeared. Just as the child slid off, the man slumped in the saddle, and then Nakaidoklinni heard the shot. In the time it takes to cut the throat of a deer so it will bleed, it was over. Two arrows pierced the front man as he sprawled face down in the water. The other had fallen from his mount, but one foot hung in the stirrup, and he was being dragged by the now panicked horse. Six warriors were in view, and one lunged for the reins of the horse, catching it as it tried to run up the narrow trail. Nakaidoklinni could not tell who caught the horse. From this distance each figure seemed to be the same naked Apache with a breechcloth, but he saw the warrior raise his lance against the hated Mexican, banishing any life that he may have harbored as his foot finally rolled from the stirrup. Nakaidoklinni could hear the terrified cries of the child, even from where he kept his vigil, as another warrior tucked the young Mexican under his arm, having blocked his path of escape. Sanchez was watching expectantly and understood as he saw his friend hold up the flat of his hand and then make a fist. All had gone just as Coyote Waits had foreseen.

"*Enju,*" thought Nakaidoklinni. It is good. This raiding path had begun with the approach of the season called Ghost Face. Each new day notched another line on the time stick he carried in his quiver, and there were thirty-four days marked so far. Coyote Waits had told the *gota* that they would return in forty days.

On Nakaidoklinni's first raid, in his fifteenth winter, the band had returned as they departed, but with emptier stomachs and poorer moccasins. Tragedy had caught them as they drove the Mexican stock into the valley of the Rio Magdalena, where they were ambushed by the Mexican cavalry. Two brave men had been killed, forcing the Apaches to abandon the herd and scatter to the hills to meet again at Big Cottonwoods Standing on the San Pedro.

The second raid followed quickly after the first so the dead could be avenged. A large herd of cattle and horses was seized, and the Mexicans paid many times for the death they had dared to inflict. Nakaidoklinni had been given a horse and three cows for his bravery and discipline, and people were heard to say that he would be a man. He was not afraid to be a raider. Coyote Waits had told how Nakaidoklinni gathered wood, made fire, cooked the horse meat, and did all that he was told. As all novices were instructed, he carefully observed and learned while seeing to the camp and doing those things the raiders had no time for. He always spoke the warpath words and always scratched with the scratching stick the shaman had given him. He always drank through the drinking tube on the amulet around his neck. He would be a warrior and a raider!

Only one more raid! One more time Nakaidoklinni would have to hold the horses, herd the stock, and keep watch for the enemy. After four raids the novice was accepted as an experienced raider who knows the names of those places on the raiding trail. One more trip and he could pull his bow with the warriors and be in the forefront of danger and not cower or run.

Someone below was signaling for the horses. Running down to Sanchez, Nakaidoklinni mounted his pony, and the boys led the others down to the white rocks where they were able to see the booty that had so recently belonged to the *nancin*. There were bolts of calico and household implements, including pots, knives, and wooden spoons. One mule was packed with three muskets with lead, shot, and molds, another with chili peppers and beans.

"Tie the horses and take those *nancin* up in the rocks. Hide their bodies well so they will not be found," directed Coyote Waits. He was wearing the white pants and shirt of the Mexican he had shot, with the bullet hole still framed in wet, sticky blood. On his head, at the same angle as his headband, was the Mexican's sombrero. He had a new rifle and a bandolier, while on his feet were a worn pair of boots.

The novice raiders carried the naked bodies up the hill, dumping them one at a time into a crevasse in the boulders. Sanchez rolled rocks down to cover the staring eyes, and Nakaidoklinni dragged brush to place over the top. They returned slowly, searching rock and sand for any blood that should be washed away. Coyote Waits said to make it look like the *nancin* had vanished so none would know that the raiding party was in the mountains. The memory of Nakaidoklinni's first raid was fresh in their minds.

Broken branches were used by the novice raiders to sweep away the sign of the ponies as the others left for the mountain camp where two other boys were left with the growing herd. Nakaidoklinni and Sanchez would meet them at dusk, meanwhile watching the rear and obliterating any signs of their passing. This they knew how to do well, for the Apache was always aware of tracks and signs that could lead the enemy and bring disaster to the band.

As the boys rode their ponies, Nakaidoklinni related what he had seen and how the Mexicans were easily surprised.

"They are like sheep," pronounced Sanchez. "The *nancin* are brave only when their bellies are full of mescal and our pouches are empty of bullets. We could kill them all if we didn't need them to give us meat or whatever we wished to take from them. They live here for us and know that we will always return and that they are like bees making honey for the Apaches."

In this he was right. The north of Sonora, all the way to the town of Hermosillo, was scattered with the bones of abandoned ranchos. Roofs were burned and caved, fruit trees were broken, and cattle were so wild that they could not be driven. These were killed and eaten when needed, but the raiders found tamer cattle to take home. When the *nancin* tried to stop the Apaches from raiding they lost their lives instead, and sometimes their women and children too.

2

I have been many times to Mexico this way when I was a young man. It is almost as if I had grown up in Mexico. From Mexico we always used to bring back lots of horses and cattle, burros and mules.

Tale of Palmer Valor, in
Western Apache Raiding and Warfare:
From the Notes of Grenville Goodwin,
edited by Keith H. Basso

The raiding party was camped in a sheltered canyon on the other side of the mountain from where the *conducta* was seized. In the summer this was an area of *tinajas,* where water could be found in rocky recesses even in dry times, but now, with Ghost Face settled on the land, a small stream watered the canyon, providing a pasture for the stolen stock. Besides the ten animals just captured, about twenty mules, sixty horses, and another sixty or so cattle were peacefully grazing. This was a good raid, and the chiefs of this party would be richer and even more respected when once back with the *Nde,* the People. Even the novices would have enough possessions after this raid to be noticed by the elders and envied by those younger than them who had not yet taken up the raiding trail. With Nakaidoklinni's and Sanchez's share of booty, parents of maidens who had passed through *nai-es,* the puberty ceremony, would start to consider that these young men might be good providers, for when men married, they joined the camp of the woman and were obligated to that *gota*.

Nakaidoklinni considered these things as he and Sanchez signaled to the other apprentices and rode into camp, turning their ponies loose to graze with the large herd. They proudly walked to the fire, where horse meat was broiling on the coals, but not being allowed to eat entrails or even warm food on the first four raids, the boys chewed their mescal and dried lung that they had prepared while guarding the herd. The lung was light, they had been told, and its air would make them swift.

While eating, Nakaidoklinni and Sanchez listened to the men talk of the day's exploits and studied the boy of six or seven winters haunched behind Coyote Waits. He wore a long Mexican coat made of cotton and had bare feet sticking out of the white *pantalones*. The fall of tears that had cascaded down his cheeks was dry, and on his face was a bloody, beaded red welt.

"This boy tries to run but doesn't watch where he goes." Coyote Waits pointed with his lips to the boy and all eyes followed his.

"¿Cómo se llama, niño?" questioned Coyote Waits.

"Yo soy Carlos," whispered the boy.

"Carlos, Carlos. This boy says his name is Carlos. He will be my slave and sleep in my *gota* and get my horse when I want to ride. He needs a name for the *Nde*. What is a Carlos? An Apache should have a name that all can understand: a name that means something. I will call him He Who Runs so his legs will get strong. He will be fast and then he can be a good warrior."

"Now, feed that boy and let him get a drink. Then tie him up so He Who Runs will still be with us tomorrow." Sanchez moved to give the boy some meat, but

he shrank back and would not eat. So they bound
him near the fire, where he would be warm throughout the chill Ghost Face night.

· · ·   · · · · · · · · · · · · ·

10   Nakaidoklinni woke before dawn; he scraped some
coals together and kindled a small fire. Gradually the
camp came to life as the warriors prepared to meet
the new day. Each man looked to Coyote Waits, won-
dering what he would decide was in store. This was
his raid. It was he who was wise in the ways of the
raid.

"You boys. There is that dead oak up there on that
ridge," said Coyote Waits, and he pointed it out with
his lips. "You run up there to urinate like coyote.
Scratch dust over that place and holler like coyote
does. That way you will be like coyote. You will be
smart in war and avoid any trouble that may come
to you."

This the boys did. They bent over and trotted like
coyote, taking advantage of cover to stop and watch
like coyote does. They looked just like coyote pups
running up there to that dead oak tree.

Nakaidoklinni ran a little further to urinate near
that place and then kicked dirt over the foamy wetness
as he heard Sanchez give a coyote yip behind him.
He did the same, and then the boys came together
near a ledge where they saw the camp sentry and
the country beyond. They enjoyed the rays of the
morning sun warming their limbs just as the turkey
vulture spreads its wings at the start of each day.
Nakaidoklinni took some *hoddentin* from the bag tied
in the fold of his moccasins and marked the forehead
of Sanchez and himself with the sacred pollen.

There were those boys high above the camp, the

Each man, including the novice raiders, was instructed to his tasks, and as warriors had done for over two hundred years, they prepared for the long, hard ride to the mountains where they lived near the $\cdot$ $\cdot$ $\cdot$
Rio Blanco.

The bounties fixed on scalps varied, a male Apache or Comanche scalp bringing at one time two hundred pesos, a female scalp or a female prisoner, one hundred and fifty pesos, and a child—to be peoned, enslaved—one hundred pesos. Generally, the bounty was lower, a prime scalp at one time being valued only at a good Mexican pony.

J. Frank Dobie,
Apache Gold and Yaqui Silver

Nightfall settled her chill blanket upon the raiding party as they drove the herd across the valley below the sheltered canyon, a frosty moon lighting the way. Apaches were not given to keeping livestock and were not shepherds to their flocks. Cattle and horses were food and raw material that furnished water skins, hides to throw over wickiups, thick tough leather stronger than deer skin, and hooves to use for glue. These animals weren't spared but were run a good part of the way back to the rancheria, at least as far as necessary to be safe from the Mexican cavalry. A slower pace could be set once safety was assured, but until then the herd was pushed hard, and each man did his part to keep the ghostly procession on a northward course at what was a controlled stampede. Slowly the Great Bear revolved in the sky, pointing the way north as other constellations rose and set.

The mountains where the herd had been gathered were far behind, with the Sierra de San Jose now looming to the east. By midmorning they should be to the valley of the San Pedro, beyond which the Mexicans would not pass because they said they had sold that land to the government of the white men. How, the young raider wondered, could they sell something that hadn't been theirs, a land they had never controlled?

Nakaidoklinni felt the rhythm of the herd as it flowed across the land, responding to yells of the raiders, the wave of a blanket, and the urging of the pressing ponies. He had packed some dried mescal, and this he chewed as he and the dusty herd melded in the purposeful oneness of moving another hill, another canyon, north. And then another. If danger threatened, the scouts would let them know. Until then each man was lost to the herd, unconsciously checking here, pushing there, with one eye on the beasts, one eye on the trees and brush, the cactus and coyote holes that presented themselves to the unwary.

Night wore on. Time was measured by the bellowing cattle as the dusty trail pulled the herd northward. From where he was, near the middle of the migrating animals, Nakaidoklinni sometimes caught a glance of Sanchez on the other side. When the clouds scudded to the east, leaving a clearer sky, he could see others ahead more to the point. They were crossing another broad plain north and west of the Dragoons, the country rolling through mesquite scrub and forests of ocotillo. A stronger wind from the west blew dust across the herd, and the bitter cold caused him to hunker close to his warm mount.

As he passed the stony outcrop of a small hill, he thought he heard a distant cadence of chanting, causing him to stir in his Apache saddle. But the sound faded and the night was just as before, though Nakaidoklinni was more alert. He flapped his blanket and observed the moon nearly overhead as its glow filtered through the layer of cloud. Once he thought something had flown in front of the moon, but it was out of the corner of his eye, and when he looked there was nothing to be seen. Had something been there, he wondered? Had something called him? He gave the pony a reassuring squeeze with his knees and tried to ignore the cold.

The moon had traveled three-fourths of the way to the western horizon when Nakaidoklinni heard it again, and the prickles on his arm made the hair lift up from his skin. From a nearby arroyo he heard a low moaning chant that sounded as if it came deep from the ancient rocks and sand. He swung his pony over that way but saw no sign of fire or man as the sounds soaked back into the ground.

That night the band had crossed the pass between the Winchester and Galiuro Mountains, bringing them into the Arivaipa Valley, where Coyote Waits called for a halt before they pushed on to the Gila. A beef was killed and cooked, this being the first meal the party had eaten since leaving the pasture where the herd had been gathered. Nakaidoklinni listened carefully to the talk as he chewed his cold meat and drank the icy water through his reed. He wanted to know if anyone else heard the chanting that had come to him in the night. It seemed that no one had. Even Sanchez had noticed nothing unusual, for Nakaidoklinni had brought up the cold and the cloudy moon, giving his friend the chance to mention anything unusual, but he only talked about where they would cross the Gila.

Coyote Waits had each man again change horses and then took them up the Arivaipa toward the Mescal Mountains and over to the Rio San Carlos at the point where its waters flowed into the Gila. Here they forded and made camp for the night, being in familiar country. Nakaidoklinni was told to be a sentry, so he rode to a small hill above the camp, taking his blanket, meat, and water with him. The sun was below the mountains, with the evening star shining in the west. Coyotes were calling from ridge to ridge but were not to be seen, though Nakaidoklinni had seen a great white wolf stalk up his pony track and stop just out of bow shot, where it sat on its haunches and watched Nakaidoklinni till the red star became visible. Then it had turned and trotted off. Never before had he seen a white wolf like that. If he had been a raider and not a novice, if he had been allowed to bring his weapons, he would have tried to shoot that wolf. Instead, he watched it disappear in the night, noting the path it took from where it had sat watching him. Maybe I'll see him again tonight, he thought. He wished he could make a fire, but that would be spotted too easily.

Nakaidoklinni knew that the men below trusted him to keep watch through the night. This was a job given to apprentices, but not just any boy would be trusted enough to risk the safety of the raiders to his alertness. He would not fail them in this, he knew in his heart. It was cold and his limbs were tired, but he would keep watch and stay awake. He remembered that wolf out there somewhere in the dark. But did he stay awake? In the morning he thought so but wasn't sure. He did know that in the night the white wolf came back to talk to him. It trotted right up the pony track, barked once, and then started making low growling sounds that Nakaidoklinni was able to understand.

The wolf talked to him and said, "I have been watching you. I saw you down in Mexico and I followed you to this place. You are a novice raider and always do what those men tell you to do. I like that. I've never seen such a novice as you. You are my kind of boy, that's for sure. You are already getting rich now even though you have only sixteen winters. Coyote Waits will give you some of those cows, some of those horses. You will have some of those knives, some of those cloths. That's for sure. I want to give you something too, because you will be a shaman and a leader of the *Nde,* and I can help you.

Nakaidoklinni looked at the wolf shimmering in the moonlight. It was a big beautiful wolf with steam coming from its mouth when it talked to him. Its yellow eyes looked at him, but he could tell they were not waiting for the right moment to jump and eat him. No, he need not fear that from this wolf, and he even wanted to touch its soft fur, which was so long and lustrous.

"What is it you can give me?" asked Nakaidoklinni. He was aware of a desire to touch the wolf, but he fought it with the caution he knew should be shown that four-legged predator.

"You can have some of my wolf power. This will be a *diyi* for you to call on when you need some help in some way, like if you want to find a horse that is lost or maybe you want to cure some tired legs when on the warpath. A boy like you can use this power to run fast. You can run from your *gowa* on the Rio Blanco to Mexico in three days and not even be tired. I have done it, just as you will be able to.

"I want you to be just like a wolf among your people. This will be good for you, and you are the only boy I can help like this. When this raid is over, take two horses to someone who can tell you about wolf power so you can learn my songs and know about the places where I live."

With that said, the wolf came right up to the novice's feet and put his front paws on his shoulders. Nakaidoklinni stood up straight, unafraid. Slowly he put his hand in that long thick white fur. Then the wolf disappeared.

In the morning, Nakaidoklinni still had wolf fur in his hand, but of the wolf tracks nothing could be seen, not even on the soft sand where he stood on his hind legs. Nakaidoklinni took out his small pouch of *hoddentin* and sprinkled some in his palm. Then, giving thanks to the day and to the wolf, he blew the pollen in frosty puffs toward the first rays of the new day.

.... **4** ...

The man I heard singing most at victory dances was Old Man
Black. He used to wear an owl-feather cap. He knew those songs
the best. But I don't know who made the songs in the beginning.
They just came down from the beginning of the Earth I guess.
                        Western Apache Raiding and Warfare:
                        From the Notes of Grenville Goodwin,
                        edited by Keith H. Basso

There was rejoicing in the winter camp when the
raiders arrived. Sanchez had been sent ahead to give
word of their return so the people could prepare for
their arrival. A feast and dance would be held that
night in honor of the successful quest to Mexico. Men
and boys came out to escort the heroes back to the
gota, back to the large extended family and clan that
claimed the raiders. Each man and each novice was
welcomed back with respect shown for their deeds
and newly won wealth.

Nakaidoklinni's mother and sisters were among a
knot of women in front of their wickiup as he drove
the herd in, preparing to divide the spoils. A festive
spirit engulfed the camp, partly because all the men
had returned safely, and also because the reality of
survival was assured by the success of the raid.

The herd was gathered together, and Coyote Waits
began to portion out the animals in a way that he
had predetermined, beginning with the mules, then
the horses, and finally the cattle. The men first cut

out all the mules, and then Coyote Waits called for each man to rope the animal of his choosing. Thus the herd dwindled as the animals were led away. Because this was his third raid, Nakaidoklinni received a larger share than he had previously gotten; that day he roped one mule, three horses, and three cows for his own.

Coyote Waits called attention to the six burros. "You six men who came on this raid and showed these boys how to take horses and cattle from the Mexicans can have these burros, one for each man. You deserve it! Go on and take them, now. I don't need one of those burros, you go ahead and take them." Saying this, he stood back to watch as each man got his burro, unpacking the goods on its back and placing them in a heap with the other stolen goods that had been unloaded from the mules. A murmur of approval coursed through the crowd as the generosity of Coyote Waits was recognized. Finally, the knives and cloth, powder and shot, blankets and saddles and other goods were also given out until nothing was left. Because it had been a successful raid, each raider was richly rewarded according to his experience and contribution. Many of the other men and adventurous boys regretted not going on the raid.

A large stack of firewood had been prepared once Sanchez arrived with word of the returning raiders. Then a fire was prepared on the dancing grounds, toward which the people gravitated that night. Word had spread to other nearby camps, and many Apaches rode in to celebrate the successful raid, some who came from as far away as the Arivaipa. Long Ears, the principal chief, gave a big speech welcoming the men back, commending them on the safe return. He, in turn, asked Coyote Waits to show his new boy, He

Who Runs, and to give an account of the journey. Coyote Waits thoroughly complied, dressed in his new clothes, which were formerly worn by the dead Mexican. Each man was called up to tell his part of the adventure, carefully dancing the drama, the heroics of his part. Coyote Waits then had two mules brought near to the fire, where he had his young son kill them with well-placed arrows. Upon this the mules were butchered and the feast began. The next day each member of the raid would select one of his animals to be killed and butchered; everyone in the camp would be welcome to take what they needed so that fresh and dried meat were available to all who had need. Thus the elderly, widowed, and divorced were cared for in the Apache camp.

For now, though, the food was enjoyed by all. When every belly was popping from mule meat, a drum was tied, signaling the arrival of *inda ke ho ndi*. Each raid ended with *inda ke ho ndi,* which meant "property of the enemies" dance. It was now that any woman could ask any of the raiders to give her whatever she wished from what they had brought back. The woman could sing for what she wanted or she could dance with the raider and he would have to pay her for the dance with whatever she demanded. Widows who might have problems supplying all the needs for their camp could get what they needed now, and might well offer more than a dance or a song. This was a time of release as the warriors were relieved of the warpath language as well as the strictures of sexual abstinence. Like a thunderstorm in summer, the Apache danced away the tension, the dangers, the cares, and the hardships that had been their lot on the raiding trail. The people who waited for their return celebrated that abundance was theirs, that their fears and concerns had come to naught. No woman would hack her hair, keening into the night, never to see her husband or son again. All was well.

· · · · · · · · · · · ·

Nakaidoklinni and Sanchez were unfamiliar with their new status. Though they were still boys, their positions had changed from being inexperienced novices to being seen as warrior candidates. As such, people saw them differently now; they were seen as young men on the path to adulthood. One more raid and they could find other promising boys to entrust with the scratching sticks that were still tied at their necks. Girls were looking at them differently, too, casting furtive glances when the boys weren't looking, or perhaps standing in their groups and suddenly laughing so that the boys self-consciously wondered if they might be the objects of the laughter. Nakaidoklinni found that everyone he talked to or passed allowed him a greater measure of respect.

"My brother, that girl they call Ilnaba keeps watching you," Sanchez told Nakaidoklinni, as they stood near the fire.

"I think it is you that she sees," murmured Nakaidoklinni, but his heart beat a little faster, for Sanchez confirmed what he had dared to hope. The girl's family was from the Cibique group and had joined his *gota* in the fall. Nakaidoklinni had not talked to her before but had inquired of her clan and knew that they were not closely related. "Let us go back and watch the dancing. I am tired of riding a horse, and it is good to be here with the people again."

But Sanchez noticed that Nakaidoklinni's eye was not for all the people but for one young maiden in particular, though, like her, he was trying not to be obvious in showing his interest.

Ilnaba had her back to them and was talking with her sister on the other side of the dancers. Her black hair, which would fall to her knees if let down, had been combed and parted, then gathered and wrapped at her neck in a long hourglass shape. She wore beautiful fringed buckskin with an extra layer of fringe sewn on the skirt. When she moved, the metal tinklers on her cape sounded like a singing brook. Sanchez was once again talking about the small herd he had won in Mexico and how he might take his horses to trade with the Zuni.

"We can go during Many Leaves. What do you say, will you go?" Turning his mind to Sanchez's question, Nakaidoklinni considered whether Many Leaves would be a good time to go to Zuni Pueblo. Many things were on his mind, including the white wolf and what he would do about wolf power. Before he could answer, he saw Sanchez's eyes raise, and Nakaidoklinni turned just in time to see a naked woman, a widow from a nearby camp, reach out and tap him on the shoulder. Nakaidokinni saw that she was much older than himself. Her face was painted, and a broad white band with black spots was painted under one arm and over the other shoulder. By the rules of the *inda ke ho ndi* he was obliged to dance with her, and when they were finished she would have the right to ask a gift of him: something from his share of the booty. Shyly, Nakaidoklinni followed her into the dancers, as they took their places in the line and surrendered to the beat of the drum and the chants of the singers. Skillfully, this woman kept trying to lead Nakaidoklinni to the edge of the dance ground, far from the fire, where paths led out to the bushes; but Nakaidoklinni's mind was on Ilnaba, to the widow's detriment. Returning to the fire, she demanded a cow for her trouble and then went off to find someone more agreeable to dance with.

Nakaidoklinni carefully stalked back around the dancers to Sanchez. "I saw you with your wife, my brother. She is very lovely, like an elk."

"Young deer are more to my liking," muttered Nakaidoklinni.

"That is too bad," replied Sanchez. "You should not have danced with the painted elk. While you were gone a young doe saw you and ran off into the darkness."

Nakaidoklinni looked, and sure enough, she was gone. All he could think was, "I must soon join another raid so I will be known as a warrior."
· · · · · · · · · · · · ·

It was in this season that the band of Long Ears received a party of Chiricahua men who were painted and dressed for war, with many guns among them. These men were on foot and had come from the mountains of the band of Cochise. This is the story told by Haske Hagola to the people of Long Ears' camp.

"My brothers, this warrior comes to you because the earth tugs at his breast. The moon has moved in the sky and the waters in the mountains have withdrawn into the sands.

"The wagons of the white man have passed through our land for many years. They come in flat wagons with blue soldiers and they come in round wagons with women and children. The Chiricahuas let them pass because they do not stay and sometimes we can trade with them. Sometimes we sell them wood or meat. We do this where they keep their horses in the corral by the spring at the place they call Apache Pass. We have followed the word of Cochise and Mangas

Coloradas and let these people go to the west where they dig the yellow metal that white men seek.

"Just now there came a troop of blue soldiers to that corral. They said they wanted a parlay, so we came from our winter camp with a white flag. Cochise went to the tent of the *nantan* lieutenant to smoke and talk, but he said he did not have tobacco for Cochise, though he had some for himself.

"The blue lieutenant said to Cochise that we must have taken a boy and some cattle from a rancho on Sonoita Creek and we had better give them all back quickly or he would imprison Cochise at Fort Buchanan. Cochise told him that we knew nothing of the boy or this raid. The *nantan* said Cochise lies, and soldiers came up to the tent to capture the Chiricahuas. Cochise drew out his knife to cut through that tent and ran to the rocks and escaped, but six Apaches did not get away. Now those men are dead, hanging from trees with ropes around their necks. Those three white men at that corral are dead too, and so are more who came down that pass in a wagon. No more will the white man's wagons be allowed to pass! No more is the white man the friend of Mangas and Cochise! These six men in the trees must be avenged! There are ranchos and mines south of the Gila near Fort Buchanan where we go to kill white men and get horses and booty."

Long Ears heard these words of the Chiricahua and listened to some men of his camp who wanted to join the war party. One man, a Chiricahua who had married into Long Ears' camp, was going to avenge his relations, and several others joined him, too. That night a war dance was held to prepare the heart and mind for war. Each man was painted with a white stripe over the nose and under the eyes, and Nakaidoklinni was one of these men. He had asked Long

Ears to be allowed to go, and Long Ears had spoken to the Chiricahua for him.

"Here is a good boy for you who has been on three raids. He can run fast and keep up and doesn't complain. You can use him to fix your moccasins or find some food when you run out. Maybe he can guard any captives you get or take care of horses." So, with Long Ears' recommendations, Nakaidoklinni was accepted, whereupon he began preparation for his fourth raid as a novice.

The war dance prepared the warrior for the rigors of combat and endurance of hardship. These men were in superb physical shape and could run all day if need be, covering as much as seventy miles in one leg. Endurance was everything, as thirst was sometimes satisfied with a pebble or stick placed in the mouth, and hunger and cold were forgotten. The mind, too, must be prepared to endure all and to react to any enemy in a warpath way.

Once the people gathered, the Chiricahuas began the dance, calling each man individually. He would then come out and dance to show how he would fight. Some carried lances and shields, but many had guns, which were fired when it was their turn. Nakaidoklinni, who could take only a bow with four hunting arrows, danced how he would guard any stolen property and keep any captured enemy from escape. This was to be his job, and it was as important as any other that must be done.

Now a cowhide was brought up to the fire. The Chiricahua war chief picked it up and danced around the fire four times, chanting and singing about enemy property he would take, beating the hide each time he got on the south side of the fire, toward Fort Buchanan. After each man did this, the social dancing began and carried through the night till dawn.

Ndi biji i jesi means a death song. Everyone knows that a warrior on the warpath might not come back. If a raider did not come back, the people mourned deeply and a pall was cast over the raid; but a warrior must expect to die and be prepared to sacrifice his life if necessary. At dawn the war party gathered together, and the Chiricahua war chief sang the death song to give each man a strong heart so he would fight bravely and not run. Because this man had "enemies-against" power, the others would willingly follow him, bravely charging into the teeth of the enemy. That man would sing that same song again when the party went into battle.

"Now is the time to go out on the warpath," said the chief. "Those white men have accused us of something we have not done. We told them we didn't do this thing, but they killed six of our men anyway. We didn't ask for this fight, but now that the white man has done this, we have to do something. You men going along are ready now. We are going down by Fort Buchanan, where the blue soldiers who killed those six Chiricahuas are. Don't be afraid to die. One of these women here can bear another son. Be brave and don't run because we will be strong if each man does his part. Stay in single file when we go down there and don't turn over any rocks or break any grass or twigs. You men have to use warpath language now because we go to fight the *nancin*. You two novices must always use your scratching sticks and drinking tubes. If any of you think impure thoughts it will threaten the war party. Just keep thinking about that cowhide dance you did and those words you sang."

Turning from the warriors, he now addressed the people: "You who stay behind, keep these men in your thoughts. Don't argue with anyone and don't speak any bad words. Have pure hearts now. Don't have any evil things going through your head." Upon this, he instructed the men to get their weapons, extra moccasins, and food. Then they departed, single file, and headed toward the fastness of the mountains, where they could see far and escape with ease.

· · · · · · · · · · · ·

Three days of travel brought the small war party to the hills overlooking Sonoita Creek, where a few ranchos were beginning to dot the landscape, taking advantage of the lush grasses and dependable water. Below the hill was a narrow valley through which the creek trailed a snaky line through stands of oak and walnut. Nestled in one of the curves of the creek was a small cabin and a pole corral bordering on a dry hay field that had been left standing through the winter. A few head of cows and horses were grazing there, along with a small flock of sheep.

A man could be seen walking back and forth from the cabin to the corral, and a haze of smoke crowned the cabin, carrying downwind across the creek. Three men were picked to steal down a canyon that would bring them out above the cabin near the field, and three more left by a different route that would place them behind the cabin on a low bluff across the creek. The other men stayed low on the hill, well under the crest on a brushy slope of jumbled granite boulders. Patiently the men watched and waited and eventually saw the three come out of the canyon above the cabin, where they took advantage of the cover until they started crawling down one side of the field away from the grazing animals.

The horses must have smelled the men in the field because first one and then the others raised their heads to look in their direction and suddenly trotted off toward the corral, where the rancher climbed a rail to see what had spooked them. As he scanned the field he sort of folded over the pole and then toppled into the corral as the men on the hill heard the sound of a shot. But the man wasn't dead; he started crawling back along the corral to the gate and then made a dash to the cabin, making it through the door even though he had been shot at five or six times. The men in the field were now in the corral, where they took up positions covering the door while a man to the rear stalked up to the back of the cabin. Pretty soon, more smoke came from the cabin as flames were leaping up to the roof, making a black smoke.

The flames kept building until the cabin door opened about halfway. Several shots were fired as smoke poured from the door. Eventually a man ran out about ten steps and then crumpled to the ground. Then there came another, crawling on hands and knees, but with a rifle. He took up behind a tree, firing toward the corral, not noticing the Chiricahuas behind the house coming toward him with a lance. Suddenly, in a rush, it was over, the lance doing its silent work. The whole party now converged on the blazing cabin, where the white men were both stripped and then shot and lanced several more times, each warrior doing his part to right the wrong done to the six Chiricahuas hung up in the trees and left to the buzzards. Two men went to the field and lanced the sheep because they were too slow to travel with a war party. Others were out catching the horses and cattle. The war chief then went to the cabin and, seizing a brand, hurled it out in the field so that quickly the hay and corral both were burning. Then the men headed north, making tracks, trying to put as much distance as possible between themselves and the carnage.

· · · · · · · · · · · ·

Nightfall brought them to the San Pedro, near the Overland Trail crossing. The war chief directed Nakaidoklinni and two others to water the stock and then continue on, driving day and night back to camp.

"In the morning the stage will come from Tucson and we will stay here to meet it. You take all those animals down through.the water so your tracks will disappear. After we stop that stage we will have more horses and then will be able to ride back and meet you."

It took Nakaidoklinni three days to return to camp. The following day the other warriors arrived, some walking and some riding on large brown mules, each of which wore the same brand. One man was missing, but a hostage had been captured. That night at the dance everyone heard the story told by the Chiricahua war chief.

"The morning after the men left with the horses and cows we could see dust coming from the west. It was some wagons. The San Pedro is sandy there where those wagons would have to cross, so we got over on the other side, up the hill where the mules would have to be lunging. We covered ourselves with cottonwood bark and waited till we heard them coming. There were two big freight wagons, each with two men, all well armed. I sang the death song as they came down to the water, where they stopped to let the horses drink; the men stood and stretched and talked. They started again pretty soon going up that sand, whipping the mules, but the sand was too deep and the front wagon got stuck. The white men talked back and forth for a while, and then the men behind unhitched their mules and brought them up to the wagon in front. There were long metal ropes that the mules used to pull the wagons, and the metal ropes of the two teams were tied so that twelve mules could pull the first wagon. They got going, all right, and came right up to where they would have to go between us. First I shot that man driving those horses, and the man next to him was hit in the arm but started shooting a long gun with two barrels. His first shot killed the man you do not see here. The second wagon was standing in the water with no mules, so it couldn't go anywhere. When the man with the two barrels had to load again, he got lanced. Those two other men were trying to run off and get away, I guess. But one was killed and we caught this one. We did this to show those white men to leave us alone. These warriors won four horses, twelve mules, and seven cattle. We won seven good guns. Those wagons only had sacks of grain, so we dumped it in the water. We took the clothes from those white men at the river and then pounded their heads in with rocks because they killed one of our men. This captive will go with us so the women of the six men in trees can dance with him all night and then kill him when the sun comes up. We didn't start this, but we will finish it."

Thus ended Nakaidoklinni's fourth raid as a novice. He got another horse and asked for a gun, which he was given. He was proud to be a warrior now and stayed up all night dancing. Once, in the embers of the fire, he could see the white wolf prowling for him. Most men waited till they were warriors before they got any powers, and now he was ready.

It must be understood that this wild section was almost terra
incognita *to any but the Indians. A few important points, such
as springs and water holes and peaks, were known to a few
hardy frontiersman and army men, but often their situation was
conjectural, indefinite.*

Thomas Cruse,
Apache Days and After

And so it goes. Apache time. One day follows another,
and soon the new moon rises, causing the seasons to
move in their cycle, for every season has birth and
death, just as the sun moves in the heavens from
north to south and back. The seasons of Many Leaves
pile up, but each season, each day, heralds the beginning of the cycle anew. Everything changes. Nothing changes.

Who can say what brought those people—the *Nde*,
the Apaches—to this place? Who can say if the desert
and the mountains made the Apaches? This was their
home, their land. Maybe they made it that way. Maybe
those other people made it that way. The ones who
built the stone houses and the ditches. The ones who
left their manos and metates and axes and arrowheads
when they moved away. The *Nde* didn't claim the
land. They lived it. The land, the rocks and streams
and mountains, had a life force. It grew trees to shade
the earth and search the sky for clouds that come to
bless the land with the wetness of the gods. Deer grew

here too. And birds. And coyotes, and snakes, rabbits, rats, antelope, cougar, and Apaches. They all grew here at the urging of the land. "Go forth and walk me. Fly above my plains and valleys. Eat the fruit of my being as you breathe the air and drink my waters. Return and tell me what you see, for I have no eyes of my own."

Apache time. This record etched in stone, told in legend, measured in sand washed to the valley, sung by shaman. One child to follow the last. Where does one generation leave off and another begin?

That is how it was. The people followed the seasons, and the earth provided. In Many Leaves the yucca and mescal send up their shoots for the people to bake. Large Leaves comes and the wild onion is picked or maybe the juniper berries ripen. Then the time of Large Fruit brings the raspberries and strawberries and wild potato to the mountains, cactus fruit to the desert. For the people live on the land and go where it tells them. Those people who came before lived in one place. Maybe the land didn't talk to them and tell them where to go. That could be why those people had to leave. If the fruit of the prickly pear cactus is ripe, go to that place. If mesquite beans are big and sweet, then go there. When it is that time Earth Is Reddish Brown, the corn is ready, the acorn and piñon nuts, the leaves to put in soups and stews, and seeds from all the grasses. The *Nde* get sunflower seeds then. Just go get them where they grow. Now is a good time to get deer. Those deer are fat now and they let you hunt them like Child of the Water did when he was on earth. When that deer is dead you say, "May I always have luck with you. Don't be afraid of me when you see me. We all are of this land, and my body needs your meat."

Who can say why those Mexican people are there? They have been there a long time. All that time they keep trying to move north to take this land the *Nde* live for. They bring their soldiers in shining metal and those black priests of the cross. They bring black men and Aztec men and other Indians from Mexico. They bring soldiers and disease to make the *Nde* die. They kill the people, take prisoners for slaves, keep them imprisoned, sell them, beat them, and cut off a hand or a foot. They say this land belongs to them. They say their king gave it to them, or their god. They give one hundred pesos for the scalp of an Apache warrior. They give less for the scalp of an Apache child. This is why when "Ghost Face" comes, *Nde* raid those Mexicans. They are *nancin* then. This is the warpath language. Who can say why the *nancin* are there? They are just like piñon trees, the cactus and the grass. They have fruit and the *Nde* use it. Apaches take those horses. They take those mules. Those *nancin* shouldn't have moved there. That is not their country. *Nde* land is not their land.

6

It was fascinating to be in the wilderness with an Apache. There was something about it that would appeal to any man, for the primitive is very close to the surface in all people.

Col. H. B. Wharfield,
With the Scouts and Cavalry at Fort Apache

Among the Apaches many people had power, and this was good. Sometimes people got sick because they drank water that a bear or a coyote had been in, so they would find someone with that power, and he could help them with a ceremony. The *Nde* had to be careful not to step where a snake had walked, and not to get sick from ghosts, but if they weren't careful with things like that they could get help from someone who knew about snake power or ghost sickness.

A warrior could be helped out if he had some extra power to call on, such as "enemies against" power, to tell where the *nancin* were and how many there were. "Enemies against" power could tell how to defeat them. Horse power was good to get too. If a herd being driven back from a raid was spooky, a man with horse power could come in there and say some words and those horses calmed right down. If raiders on a war party were being pursued, wind power could be called on to make a big wind and a lot of dust to help the party get away. Some men had running power and could run long distances without even getting tired. They might run while they said "closer, closer," and wherever they needed to get would be closer right away. Women could have these powers too, and many of them did. Lozen, the sister of Victorio, could see enemies from far away and tell in what direction they were. She just stood up and held out her fingers while she turned around slowly, and she could tell every time! Because of this, and because she was a good fighter, she went on many raids and war parties.

Not everyone wanted a power because sometimes you had to pay for it and sometimes it would turn against you. But lots of people went out to get it anyway. You could just decide to go get some of that power if you wanted to, and maybe it would come to you on its own, or you might need to find someone who already had it and would tell you how to get it.

Sometimes the power would find a good man or woman that it wanted to help, and this is what happened to Nakaidoklinni. That wolf watched him grow up and liked what he saw. That boy was not afraid of anything and quickly learned all about bows and arrows. He was good with a spear and could ride a horse like he was born on one. He could track well, too, and when people told the boys to go break the ice on the water and swim to make them strong, he would be the one to go in first.

Nakaidoklinni didn't remember his own father but had been told about him many times and knew the story by heart. His father had been captured in Mexico when he was a little boy and had been brought back to be raised by the *Nde*. Because of this he could always speak that language and sometimes this helped them in raids, so he was often asked to go along. But he was killed by Mexican soldiers just after Nakai-doklinni was born. That white wolf knew this and for this reason wanted that boy to have some wolf power. He hunted Nakaidoklinni when he was on that third raid because he would be a warrior soon enough.

An old man named Nasta, who was of the *dosh-to-a* clan, lived in the summer at a place called White Rocks Fall Down. It was to this place that Nakai-doklinni went one day in the season of Large Leaves after he became a warrior. By now he had given most of his horses and cows away to people who needed meat, but he had kept back the five best horses. This day he had brushed and combed two of them and cleaned their tails of burrs and thistles, and now he was leading them toward the place White Rocks Fall Down, where he was directed to the wickiup of Hastin Nasta. He tied the two horses to a bush near the hut where Nasta lived and then patiently sat his horse, awaiting the old man to recognize him. The flap of the wickiup was thrown back, for the day was warm, and soon Nakaidoklinni saw a white head and wrinkled neck emerge. Nasta greeted Nakaidoklinni and motioned him over to a brush-covered arbor where they both seated themselves on some cowhides.

"My eyes have faded, my son, but do I know you?" asked the old shaman.

Nakaidoklinni shook his head. "I am of the camp of Long Ears. I am of the White Water people and my father was Nak-ai-tulan." Saying this, the young warrior had identified who he was. It would be for someone else to tell Nasta his name. Names were not used face to face but only when speaking of a third person.

Nasta now inquired of the camp of Long Ears, asking about many of the people of Nakaidoklinni's acquaintance. From here they had a long conversation about the game, the crops, the weather, and the winter's raids to Mexico, and now Nakaidoklinni was able to tell of his experiences in attaining the status of warrior. Nasta listened without expression and then told of a raid he had made to Mexico when he had been a young man.

"It happened long ago," he began. He told of a raid he had made down the Rio Sonora. They had followed the stream bed until it met the Water That Meets the Sky, and they were all glad because of their thirst. "But we were tricked by Coyote, who got there before us and put salt in all the water so we could not hold it in our mouths. So we just walked there along the water and everywhere we stepped was like snow, so we looked, and it was shells. We all got some, and I still wear mine here," and he reached to the string at his neck. "Because these come from the water, I wear them so that the rains will always come."

Nakaidoklinni waited till the old man was finished and then brought out his small pouch of wolf fur, saying, "I too have something I brought back from a raid to Mexico." Then he told of the chanting in the night and the visit with the white wolf.

"Yes," said Nasta. "That wolf was hunting you. Stay with me till the next moon and I will help you get the wolf power that it wants you to have."

. . . .

That is how it happened that Nakaidoklinni stayed with the old shaman Nasta. It was not only until the new moon that he stayed, though, but for three moons, so that when he at last rode back home it was again the season Earth Is Reddish Brown and the people of Long Ears' band had left to gather the sweet acorns that grew by the place called Ash Flat.

Nasta had told him about wolf power, all right! Each day the two were together, Nasta would talk about the power of the wolf and how it could be used. He would talk like this: "To have wolf power that you can call on, you must always be able to see what the wolf sees and think like a wolf thinks. Everything that *Nde* see, Wolf sees too. Everything that *Nde* does, Wolf does too. Wolf eats and drinks. Wolf fights. Wolf makes young and raises them. Wolf finds a different place to be when danger lurks. Wolf cures himself when he is sick. See what Wolf does and learn from him." Every day Nasta would talk like this and then ask Nakaidoklinni what a wolf would do if this happened or if something else happened. Nasta started teaching his wolf songs, one by one, while Nakaidoklinni learned to sing them too. And soon it was time for the new moon, but Nasta did not send the boy away. The old shaman sensed that there was something more to the boy than met the eye, and that it was not enough for this young warrior to get some wolf power and then bound off or lope back up the trail that he had arrived on. Nakaidoklinni had listened to all the words that Nasta knew and did as he was bid and gave Nasta the two fine horses, so the young man had that which he had sought and the man had been paid for that which he had given. But in the dark of the night, when his old bones wouldn't let him sleep, it would come to Nasta that there was more that he must give to the young warrior, Nakaidoklinni. So the boy stayed.

Then one day a man who had a sick wife came for Nasta to see if he would come away and cure the

woman. Quickly the shaman gathered up his medicines, rattles, and sacred objects so he could hurry
off, and it was natural that Nakaidoklinni go too,
for they had been constantly together for more than
a moon.

When they came to the wickiup of the sick woman,
perhaps ten or twelve people were there too, all concerned for her fate. The woman was on some skins
inside the wickiup, and the first thing that Nakaidoklinni noticed was that she was very flushed. They
were told that she had been hot and sweating for a
day and a half. Nasta asked that his bag of hoddentin
be given to him, then blew a pinch of it in each of
the four directions. Then he looked into the woman's
eyes and nose, feeling and smelling her breath as he
did so. With slow circular motions he felt all over her
body while softly chanting to himself. As this was
happening, all the people gathered there for the sick
woman entered the wickiup and sat around, talking
in hushed tones or just watching the shaman. To one
of these, a stooped and wrinkled old woman, Nasta
gave a few directions, and later she came back with
some red bark, which was then ground and mixed
with water. This was placed by the fire and kept warm.

It sure helps, when a shaman is making a cure and
giving a sing, to have others singing too, so Nasta
picked a couple of men who could do that for the
woman. Then he went ahead and started helping her.
He stayed there for the next four nights, chanting
and singing and shaking rattles. Every so often that
woman would have some of that liquid given to her,
and then she would always throw it up and be given
some fresh cool water. Afterward, Nasta would place
a peeled stick in her mouth, which she kept there
while the singing and chanting continued.

On the last night the woman was flushed, hot and dry. Her eyes already did not blink. Each chant, each beat, brought a leaden measure of gravity to the somber hut, and the wrinkled old woman wondered if the sick woman should be taken outside so her spirit could leave and the wickiup not have to be burned. A few twigs were added to the fire to keep it going during the night, and these cast their light in the wickiup, now flaming, then just glowing embers till more were added again. When the light was bright enough to see by, Nasta noticed that Nakaidoklinni had fallen into a deep trance. His eyes stared at nothing and his gourd rattle kept cadence to a beat that only Nakaidoklinni was aware of as it picked up and then slowed, softening nearly to an echo. He was with the wolf again. It walked on the walls when the light was dim and retreated to the flames when new wood was added. The fire was deep, the wolf far inside, casting about, ears alert, tongue dripping. Suddenly it howled, and then, nose down, running to the edge of the fire, it peered right out at Nakaidoklinni. The rattle faded to nothing as the boy rose, still with the fixed stare, and sang:

Wolf, you found me.
You followed me from Mexico.
I saw you in the fire.
You hunted me.

Wolf, you said to get your power
That I should be like you.
So come on and help me now.
I call forth your power.

This he sang four times, turning a different direction each time, and then he put a pinch of the sacred pollen in the fire and on the head of each person there, starting with that of Nasta. When he was finished, he placed a yellow dot on the forehead of the sick woman and put a little more on the bark water prepared for her. Then, with a yucca spoon, he gave her some more of the mixture to drink. This time she kept it down, and the old woman felt her body and said it was cool again, as it should be. Then they looked for Nakaidoklinni, but he was gone, and when Nasta went out he was under a tree in deep sleep, his small pouch of wolf fur clutched in his grasp. Nasta could see that Nakaidoklinni's eyes were jumping under the lids.

When they went back to the wickiup of Nasta, the old man started training Nakaidoklinni in the uses of herbs, bark, and powders that he had learned about in his long life. First he told Nakaidoklinni to take a bow and four arrows and bring back the skin of a large buck and also to take a rope, which he was to use to catch one of that year's fawns. It could not be shot but should be killed without leaving a mark, and Nasta told him how it must be skinned.

It was by now the season of Large Fruit, with warm, bright mornings and rainy afternoons. It was the season of lightning shooting from the floating cloud world. Yucca fruit were ripening, and the summer rains brought forth a bumper crop of mushrooms of the kind nipped by deer almost as soon as they popped out of the ground. So Nakaidoklinni rode to a valley known for its acorns, because the mushrooms the deer liked grew near oaks. With him he brought his bow and quiver with four arrows, a braided buckskin rope, and a deer head mask. The latter belonged to Nasta. It was the head of a male deer that had been skinned whole and then stuffed full of dried grasses so it would hold its shape. The antlers were secured on, one having two points and the other three. Two holes had been slit at the base of the neck and a loose thong threaded through.

· · ·

44   As he rode, Nakaidoklinni was overwhelmed with the force of life around him. This was the season of growth, when the world laid in fat to help get through the lean seasons. Trees, shrubs, bushes, grasses, ants, birds, all were busy growing. Did Nakaidoklinni stop to think, "This grows for me?" Did he consider that something indefinable had set this all in motion? Did he reflect that he was just another animal growing on that summer day, living out a life cycle? Who can say what he thought. Maybe he just hunted for deer. But eventually he became aware of the smell of smoke, a dark, pitchy smell like that which sometimes wafts from the old wood of a big cone tree, and soon he saw smoke smoldering from one of the ancients of the forest. A massive pine that had stood sentinel for the cycle of its life had presented too clear a target to a bolt of lightening. The tree looked as if a giant hand had reached out, grabbed it, and given it a twist. Old branches were broken in the giant's grasp, and the wood and bark that had been coiled before had been opened a bit by the tremendous twist that reversed the pattern of growth. He guided his pony around the tree and got off to examine a jagged piece of white heartwood that had been blown out of the guts of the old tree. "What kind of power," he thought, "can do this?" Not sure if it was safe to even be there in that place, he rode on, keeping the heavy, wet wood.

The valley of the oaks and mushrooms was near now, so Nakaidoklinni left his pony and crept up to a vantage point where the valley's panorama was spread below. The sun was more than halfway across the sky. Mountains of white clouds were blowing in, forming up; some were starting to turn angry and dark. Booming reverberations of thunder sounded to the north, blowing in with a fresh, wet breeze. Nakaidoklinni watched for a long time and could see three deer grazing, and an occasional neck or ear of others that were bedded down under trees. "Maybe a fawn is here," he said to himself.

Returning to the pony, he unfastened the deer head, grabbed the rope, and got two sticks a little longer than a forearm, then made his way to a thicket leading down to the deer. Well before he could possibly be seen he fitted the deer head on top of the back of his head, using the loose cord to fasten it on. Then, bending over and using the two sticks for front legs, he started to graze ever so slowly, drifting to the deer, into the breeze. Slowly, slowly, every fiber of his being attuned to being a deer, he worked down toward the resting herd, head down, grazing, till finally some deer were in view. He saw that more deer were up now, as the sun had been darkened by the clouds, and three fawns were grazing and playing, jumping at each other and then running back to their mothers to nurse. One doe had twins, and Nakaidoklinni decided on working his way, as best he could, in her direction, checking his rope to make sure the coils were untangled.

When Apaches stalk deer like this they become a deer. The head is down; movements are smooth and unhurried. They walk over to a bush with good grass and stay there awhile, occasionally looking up. Then, head down, they move on to the next bunch of grass or tasty leaves or mushrooms. Only by an accident would a deer graze in a straight line, so Nakaidoklinni zigzagged in fits and starts down toward that doe with apparent purposelessness but always making sure the wind was at his head. He got so close to her that he could have closed the distance in just four or five paces, but he kept on grazing, watching out of the corners of his eyes and with his ears for those fawns, ever so carefully shaking out the loop in his rope so it was just the right size.

The fawns were still playing and frisking about. Nakaidoklinni could hear their little hooves as they jumped and ran, slid to stops, dodged, and jumped again. They were moving away from him for the moment, but then his ears told him they were running back. Keeping his head down, he turned his neck to get a side view as one fawn ran up to the far side of its mother and took a quick pass at the nipple, sucking noisily. This brought the other twin up to the other side and gave Nakaidoklinni the chance he needed. His rope was ready, and when that fawn lifted its head, it was snared and in a smooth motion reeled in. By now, Nakaidoklinni had thrown off the deer head mask, quickly grabbing an ear and a back leg, bringing the fawn down with his weight. A quick snap of the neck, a trembling quiver, and Nakaidoklinni had an unmarked fawn, which he proceeded to skin as Nasta had said. When finished, he wrapped the loin and hindquarters in the hide, walked back to the pony, and started back to camp just as the fresh wind brought the first patter of what turned out to be a noisy, thunderous drencher that was full of hail.

Nakaidoklinni sought shelter for his pony and himself under a gnarled juniper tree whose trunk must have been as far across as a man is tall. Here he waited out the storm, still getting soaked, but at least protected from the balls of pelting ice that had built up on the ground to the depth of a walnut. He had

been there quite a while, waiting for the storm to abate, when a movement on the grassy ridge above caught his eye, and there was an old buck with odd, misshapen antlers, slowly ambling downhill, head drooping as it suffered through the hail. It was headed
for a small thicket where it, too, could find shelter. With practiced motion, Nakaidoklinni nocked his arrow and, holding the bow sideways, for it was a long shot, loosed the arrow. Another was quickly strung in its place, but it would not be necessary, for the deer was down and dead before Nakaidoklinni got to it. This he skinned also, storing the meat in the limbs of old man juniper. Then he returned the way he had come, seeing that the fire in the big pine had been quenched in the storm. So Nakaidoklinni returned to the hut of Nasta, having accomplished that which had been set for him.

Each day, more was imparted to the younger man in the arts of curing. Each day the skins of those deer evolved from what they had been. Nakaidoklinni learned to make splints of willow twigs or flat pieces of sotol while those hides were being fleshed. For the two days that they were soaking, he was instructed in treating chills with infusions of herbs, grasses, and crushed root. As the deer hair was scraped off while draped over a pole, Nakaidoklinni began to understand when pains could be sucked out of the body. With those hides pegged out over grass to dry, Nasta told him to mix pine pitch and grease for frostbite. Warm brains were worked into the buckskin while Nakaidoklinni was given to know how the sacred *hoddentin* had been provided to the *Nde*. While the buckskin was finished by pulling and stretching, Nakaidoklinni memorized all the rituals and precautions of the sweat bath just as they had been handed down long, long ago by Child of the Water. Nakaidoklinni could chant the prayer song that men sang while inside, and Nasta sang other sweat songs that he had learned. Nakaidoklinni had been shown how to use juniper smoke, cinquefoil root, sage, shavings from oak root, and Apache plume.

Now that buckskin was finished. The skin captured from the big deer was made into a medicine shirt. Nasta had ground paints, which Nakaidoklinni used to paint designs of the Apache spirit world, and the first he made was of a white wolf. Also represented were the four directions, the sun and a crescent moon, lightning and rain, and a rainbow. To this Nakaidoklinni would add throughout his life as other aspects of nature were revealed to him.

From a round piece of the little deer's hide Nasta cut a thin, continuous cord as long as four men. This he twisted together to make four shorter pieces, each longer than an arm, each a different color. Now he took long shavings from the lightning wood that Nakaidoklinni had found and encircled them in buckskin so that he had a small hoop four fingers wide. To this he tied both ends of the four buckskin braids and above them two eagle feathers.

"My son, take this medicine cord I give you. Wear it over your shoulder, across your heart. When you find that something wants to help you cure, get some of that and tie it on this cord. That way it will know that you want it to help you. This will be sacred to you, and no one else will touch it or it will be no good. So take good care of it and it will go with you and take care of your life." So saying, Nasta gave the story of his medicine cord festooned with a snake rattle, hawk claws, petrified wood, two crystals, a chip of turquoise, shells he had brought from Mexico, and a small mysterious pouch of something. Each of these had a story to tell of how they had entered the old medicine man's life and how they came to be strung on his medicine cord.

As his callused old hands had worked the new cord, he got Nakaidoklinni to make himself a medicine hat, this from the neck of the fawn. The skin was cut, leaving a scalloped tail hanging down the back. The front was rolled along the bottom edge and stitched with sinew. Another circular piece of buckskin was cut and stitched to the top, thus enclosing it. Nakaidoklinni applied a design to the hat, again starting with the wolf and then lightning. This, too, he was to continue decorating throughout his life.

Finally, taking a piece of the lightning wood, Nasta shaved it flat and made it into a rectangle as long as his hand and two fingers wide, leaving a neck sticking up on top through which he drilled a hole. On one side he carved a series of deep grooves like the V shape of vulture wings, painting some blue, others yellow. After tying another twisted cord to it, he tested it by whirling it round his head. To his delight it made a loud hum varying in pitch as it rotated toward Nakaidoklinni and then back away.

"I have made that *tzi-ditindi* for you," Nasta said, handing it to Nakaidoklinni. "Use this to call the spirits. Use this to ask the wind to bring rain or to blow away the snow clouds when it is too cold. It can talk to the sky gods because it had that lightning in it."

Thus, over the course of three moons, Nasta prepared the young shaman. As the teachings of the ways of Apache medicine proceeded, Nakaidoklinni developed his knowledge of the power of the earth and sky to cure. As the roots, bark, and leaves could be called upon to heal, so could the wind and lightning, the sun and moon. And so could the sacred pollen of the tule, the crystals of rocks, the powers of all the life that existed, that was able to animate, live, breathe, and grow. These could be called upon when sickness or injury came, when all was not as it should be. Nasta knew of these things, and as that knowledge also grew in Nakaidoklinni, so did the bond between those two men. Though Nakaidoklinni had never had a father, and though the sons of Nasta now lived with the families of their wives, that which was between the two men was not like that which is between father and son. Perhaps that was right because both of these men were men. Both had trodden paths that crossed for a time, so they shared fire and food and the things that were theirs to give. But do not conclude that Nakaidoklinni went away the richer man, for Nasta, too, was rewarded in this three-moon journey. Every old man senses his passing, often embracing it. Yet there is, in a life well lived, that which should be carried on. In this, the young warrior was as a torchbearer to Nasta.

So it was with a heavy heart, a heart on which the shaman tugged hard, that Nakaidoklinni rode off one brilliant day in the season of Earth Is Reddish Brown. Watching him go, Nasta whispered, "He sure got more than just that wolf power that he came for. He will need everything he got and maybe more."

You know, General, that we do things in war that we do not do in peace.

Cochise, in General O. O. Howard,
*My Life and Personal Experiences
among Our Hostile Indians*

Nakaidoklinni returned to a valley resplendent in the radiance of a turquoise sky and golden cottonwoods. Slowly he rode through camp, displaying his hat and medicine cord, communicating his new knowledge, and, he hoped, appearing unassuming. His mother was in the mountains gathering acorns, so he cared for his horse and walked to the camp of his friend Sanchez, where he was welcomed for the while.

Sanchez greeted Nakaidoklinni silently, and the two of them toured the camp, feeling out the other to see if anything had changed. Soon Sanchez was satisfied of the old familiar relationship and fell back to baiting his friend.

"My brother, I see you are a shaman now. Perhaps I can pay you to sing for my horse who has a bellyache."

"Leave him be until you see if he runs faster," Nakaidoklinni advised. "If not, keep your property and just jam a reed up his ass." Sanchez had a very fast pony but could rarely beat Nakaidoklinni's little paint.

Later, regaining his boldness, Sanchez inquired if his cousin could help in another direction. "You probably have forgotten that plain girl called Ilnaba of the Cibique people. Maybe I want to have that girl, but when she walks by she doesn't see me. Perhaps you can give me some love magic."

"That might be done, but you have to pay to get love magic from me, and it doesn't always work on a plain girl like her."

"If you help, I have a good knife for you," grinned Sanchez.

"Okay, then, I will help you, but you must do everything I tell you and she will notice you for sure. Do I have your word?"

"Just so, my brother. You can trust me as I trust you."

"Then here's what you must do. First pull out all of your eyebrows and all the hair from the tail of that slow horse with a bellyache. Then kill two skunks, carefully take out the scent sacks, and rub one over your horse and the other over yourself. Then ride around her wickiup with a necklace of the *manzanas* dropped by ponies. She will be sure to notice you."

At this both men laughed, and Nakaidoklinni was forced to do some unceremonious ducking as Sanchez launched several *manzanas* in his direction, thus paying for his advice.

Soon Nakaidoklinni's mother returned with her sister's family. Nakaidoklinni moved back home now and helped with the heavy work. When there was nothing else to do, he would join a hunting party if they needed venison. Everywhere he was, though, he saw Ilnaba, if not with his eyes then with his mind. At all times of the day or night suddenly there she was in his mind's eye, freshly combed hair framing her wide eyes, the oval face. There was a suppleness to her erect posture, a wholesome full-breasted plumpness. She walked with grace on small feet, and her hands, too, were small, though strong.

Yet most of his encounters with Ilnaba were confined to his thoughts, and he often took steps to avoid her presence because of his shyness. But even avoidance can be noticed by equally shy maidens and seen for what it is, so it should not be surprising that when a group from the village organized to pick corn, Nakaidoklinni, leading his horse, fell in next to the Cibique girl as if they had agreed to work together. And maybe it is not so surprising that she accepted his help, picking the corn, tying the ears, passing them to the young man to drape across his pony till a load was made. They then walked back to camp, unloaded the horse, and returned to the fields. Yet neither spoke throughout the day, and when one was looking, the other glanced in another direction.

After that time in the cornfield, Nakaidoklinni didn't avoid her so much. Often when they met or passed each other, one would make a comment like "The days sure are getting short," or "Those last hunters sure got lots of meat," or "Soon it will be time to raid to Mexico." These would be just passing comments, and maybe it was just the imagination of the hearer that made them sound like other than ordinary tones of voice.

It was Ilnaba who commented about the raids to Mexico, and the young warrior was surprised because his mind was already tending to that direction. The stock and booty he had won the previous winter were long gone. His pony and the few personal possessions he owned were all that he had. He could not expect people to give him much as a medicine man because for several years he would primarily assist older, more experienced men. If he wanted more than he had, the best route available to him was to join another raid. So this is what he did. That winter there were two good raids he joined, one to the Pima villages and one to Mexico.

In the first raid, a man had an arm broken by a bullet. Just as Nasta had taught him, Nakaidoklinni cleaned the wound and made a splint of dry, shaved sotol slats. The other warriors were sure to notice his quiet competence, and when they returned to camp everyone soon heard who had made that man's arm better. For his medicine, Nakaidoklinni had been given a gray mule, which was immediately slaughtered. Half was cut in long strips, then laid out on bushes to dry. The rest was given away.

On the raid to Mexico, the men were gone for two moons and won lots of horses and cattle. Nakaidoklinni was a warrior now, his novice days gone forever. One night they raided a village that had a lot of mules in a corral right in the middle of things. The night was bright with a good moon, and the Apaches knew it would be dangerous to walk into that corral because they might be discovered. As they watched the pueblo, discussing what to do, Nakaidoklinni said, "You men wait here till I give you the signal." Then he just walked like a wolf right down the middle of the road. When he got to the corral he took down the poles and gave the signal, so each man came down to rope a mule. Then Nakaidoklinni led them out across the river, where they mounted and rode off. Only one dog had barked, so his wolf power sure worked!

Nakaidoklinni knew that he was a wolf when he walked into that corral. Effortlessly he flitted down the street, padding on silent feet in the cool dust. Every muscle, every sense was honed to razor sharpness, working on its own and yet together. His nose separated the dung from stale tortillas, smoke from warm mule scent. Everywhere his eyes took in at once, using pale moonlight to probe every alley, each doorway, fixing dogs in their sleep, searching out the unexpected. Each ear waited to receive any sound that dared violate the silence of the Ghost Face night. He was a wolf in his bowels, wolf in the bone.

· · · · · · · · · · · · ·

A storm cloud of dust rode with them from Mexico. The *Nde* could see that a great raid had been made even before a messenger arrived to prepare for the dance of welcome. Word spread up and down the camps to wash the hair, put on finery, and prepare to celebrate. They said the men had captured a large herd of horses, mules, cattle, and burros. This was true. They also found blankets, clothing, cloth, and metal that could be made into knives, lance points, arrowheads, or the tinklers that Apache women liked to clamp to the fringes of their dresses. They got lots of saddles and bridles, too, so many presents would be made, and people came from all around.

Nakaidoklinni got a good share from this raid and was rich again. That night he danced the part he had played, everybody seeing how a wolf had stolen into a Mexican pueblo, unbarring a corral and then leading a herd of mules out of town under the noses of the sleeping Mexicans. Then he gave away many of the things that had been captured by him in Mexico.

During the social dance that evening, Ilnaba tapped him out to dance and demanded an embroidered blouse and some thin metal, and he gave her a *reboso* that had been saved with her in mind. Then they stayed together, away from the fire, out a ways in the bushes, standing well apart, mostly in silence. More was said with the eyes than with the tongue, and the chilling breeze was ignored as long as possible, after

which the young people moved back to the fire. Ilnaba did not dance with another that night, and
Nakaidoklinni only when he was tapped out so a
woman could demand a gift from him.

From that time on, the people who noticed these
things saw the young man and maiden together more
often, walking here, sitting there, usually in silence
because both were shy. That spring Nakaidoklinni
was seen helping that Cibique girl plant corn in a
plot her family was using.

"I do this for you," he told her, "because you are
always on my mind. When this corn comes up I will
help you get the weeds. If it needs water I will come
with you. You won't have to ask for me. I will be there
when you want to water that corn, that's all. I do this
for you because you are always before me and I see
you everywhere I go." He spoke as he carried a skin
full of seeds. Every so often she would reach in to
take another handful to go in the holes she had made
with her stick.

When the corn was ankle high, a brother of Nakaidoklinni's mother came one day to the wickiup of
that Cibique family. Ilnaba's mother and father were
outside by a shade they had built where he was making
arrows as she peeled the devil's claw she needed to
make baskets.

"My family would like to have that girl of yours for
our boy," he explained. "They are together all the
time, and he helped her plant your field. If you give
her to us then we can help each other like that all
the time. So we would like to have her."

The girl's mother said to him "We have a good girl,
all right. She is strong and healthy and has brought
no shame upon her family. We want to get a good
husband for her, so we will let you know."

This being said, Nakaidoklinni's uncle returned to his sister to report what was said. They well knew that the Cibique family would have to discuss this with their people. When families joined in marriage, each could benefit by getting wider kinships and more clan affiliation. But in their son's case, his father was Mexican and brought no extended family from his side, so this would have to be considered by the maiden's people. This was part of the whole question. In the balance would be the kinships, the standings of the two families, and the personal qualities of the young man who would belong to the Cibique family. They certainly would want a good provider and one not known to be lazy.

In due time the deliberations were made, with the family of the maiden signifying a willingness to favor the union and participate in the ceremony. Word was given that the marriage could go forward, and a round of gift giving began. To the father of Ilnaba three horses, three cows, and a good Mexican saddle were given. Other presents were given too: some large buckskins, some dried meat, and a gun. The horses, saddle, and cows were paid for the bride, and the other things were given out by the Cibique family to members who they knew would give back in equal value. As these presents were made, the maiden and her mother built another wickiup nearby so the young husband could easily avoid his mother-in-law, as was the custom. In a moon, when all was complete, the girl was sent to sleep in the camp of Nakaidoklinni's mother for four nights. Each night she slept near Nakaidoklinni's mother; this was done to help the young people because they were shy and didn't know what to do. On the fourth day she arose and led her husband's horse back to her mother's camp to the new wickiup. Here to help them get used to the new state, Ilnaba and Nakaidoklinni slept with her brother and one of his cross cousins. The cousins slept in the middle with the young lovers each on the outside. After four days they were left to themselves, as a married couple, to work out their shyness and awkwardness in their own way.

... 8 ....

*We found eight bodies . . . all of these scalped except one, who
had a luxurious suit of long black hair which may or may not
have been the reason of their failure to scalp him. One of the
bodies was in a sitting posture, reclining a little backward against
a bunch of cacti to which he had been bound and burned. All of
the body was not consumed and it was still partially supported
by some of the unburned thongs.*

Daniel Ellis Connor,
Joseph Reddeford Walker and the Arizona Adventure

Brown tassels crowned the tall corn now, and long
silks peered from ears that were ripening in the warm
days, the cool nights. The rains had been good to the
land so that squash and pumpkins grew in abundance,
and few could recall a time when so many acorns and
piñon nuts had been given to the people. Fat deer
ran in the woods so that hunting parties kept the
bushes near each *gowa* laden with drying meat or
scraped hides as each family prepared for the long,
lean season ahead. A rhythm of life spoke to the
people, and they responded in harmony with the
earth, a part of the oneness to which all belonged.

In her breast Ilnaba gushed and flowed with the
fullness of life now that she was a married woman
with a separate home. She, too, had grown from a
seed to be nurtured by the earth, and as she slowly
reached maturity there was a swelling and a ripeness
about her. A sweet essence of fruition enveloped her,

signifying a growth from the shy, skinny girl to the shy but proper maiden, to her new role in life as wife of a warrior and a shaman. She was ready to be that which Ussen had intended her to be. She was a ripe cook, a ripe preparer of skins, a ripe gatherer of mescal. She was a ripe harvester of corn, a ripe builder of the wickiup, a ripe weaver of baskets, and in her ripeness she could do all of those things that an Apache woman was expected to do as part of her fiber and her being.

Her mother and the other women of her clan had long noted that their daughter was an attentive, obedient girl who was quick to learn. Whenever work was to be done, Ilnaba had always been around, hanging back and silently watching until she could see what was to be done. Sometimes it was only later, after the work was finished, that anyone noticed that she had been there helping to put in the last stitches, or maybe poking the last kernels of corn down the holes or carrying the last tray in which to dry the pounded mescal. When White Painted Woman helped Ilnaba's body to be that of woman, the young Apache maiden was not unprepared. Confidently, she was able to tan, cut, and sew the doeskins that were given to make the dress for her ceremony of womanhood. Of course, her mother and grandmother were prepared to do this for her, but Ilnaba saw to it that they assisted her in making her dress instead of the other way around. She was not hard or proud about this, but rather confident and competent as she quietly went about her tasks. Her mother had used her own time to plan for all the food and to carefully consider all of the gifts that would be given. Much time was spent visiting clan members who had cloth or clothing, metal or utensils, horses or other livestock that had been won in raiding Mexicans, because these things were expected to be given to help support the *nai-es* that would be held for her daughter. Ilnaba's grandmother had sat with her as she made the dress, and as the girl finished each stage of the jacket and skirt the old woman sang her blessing while tying on amulets that she had prepared. It was the grandmother who put most of the tinklers on the dress, and she did it in such a way that when her granddaughter ran or walked during the *nai-es,* the dress sang with her graceful, flowing motion. Now, four years later, Ilnaba still walked in grace, and her husband still heard music as she busied herself about her tasks.

The young shaman was also ready for his place in his own wickiup, away from that of his mother. He felt the change in the rhythm of his life, and it was to his liking. He found himself still doing the things he had done before as the man of his mother's wickiup, but now he did those things for Ilnaba, and a new purpose, a new dedication inspired his actions. This was the way a man should be, and it had always been so. A man is born and lives and dies, and another takes his place under the sun to carry on. He hunts and eats and raids and has a family, and then he too leaves his body and passes to the world of shadows. So it had been since the dark reaches of time.

It was at this time that the rock underlying the land shifted slightly, and Nakaidoklinni felt the waters that flowed under the sands begin to spread and meander in a new way so that the trees, the game, and the very sky appeared different, but only by hue, only by subtle shades or barely discernable tone. He knew that he was not the only one to notice this because one morning Long Ears called the people together to hear his daily instructions, and the sound of his words came to Nakaidoklinni's ears differently from before.

"You people have done a good job of raising that corn this year," he said. "Those squash are fat and each vine has produced many. We have gone out and killed lots of deer, and that meat is drying and those hides are being worked. There is much mescal put aside, and the storage wickiups and ground caches are full of acorns, piñon nuts, sunflower seeds, and dried cactus fruit.

"Today and tomorrow, until the work is done, we need to get all of that corn in. Some of you should bake corn in an underground pit, and some of the corn should just be dried to make piñole. And don't forget to save some for seed because you will need to plant next year and you have to have seed.

"All of you people should work together now. Don't be lazy! Don't hold back and think that we have enough and that you have done your part, because there are still things that have to be done. You men, don't just walk off and start planning your next raid to Mexico. Help your women if they ask you to do something, because getting that corn in is hard work."

Usually when Long Ears made his morning talk he just stood in one place and said what he had to suggest to the people that day. This time, though, he kept looking off to the distance and paced, and when his steps halted, so did his words.

"This harvest has been good for us. Maybe the next harvest will be too. But don't you people get fat and think that the land will always provide as it has this time. Maybe next year the rain won't come so well. We never know how many deer there will be next year either. If it is wet and cold during the moon of

Little Eagles, we might not have so much dried fruit from the cactus."

Now he paced some more, not speaking any words, just looking off to the top of the far hills or maybe to something he saw in the clouds, but Nakaidoklinni did not see anything out of the ordinary to attract his attention. Some people thought that Long Ears had said what he had in mind and had forgotten to tell them to return to their tasks, but nobody left yet. Nakaidoklinni could see some of those around him turn to search the hills behind them, and maybe look up at the clouds, but then they turned around and once again settled their eyes on the enigmatic frame of Long Ears.

"You people know that those wagons of the white man have been going toward the setting sun for a long time now. The first time I heard of this I was a young warrior, and some of us went to see what this was all about. There were eight of those wagons that were round on top, being pulled by big brown mules. We watched them go until only their dust could be seen, but always they kept going.

"You people have heard of the white men who came to the Gila River to take the skins of beaver and otter. Our brothers from the Pinal Mountains saw them, and some of them were killed by those white men. But some white men were killed too. And then those white men left and were never seen again.

"After that, one time some men came here from the camp of Mangas Coloradas. They said that white men had been over there and had bought some land from Mexico and were there to see where the boundary was. Those men said that Mangas told those white men that this land never was held by the Mexicans and that after the white men stayed for two moons, they left and were never seen again.

"After that, five harvests ago, blue soldiers came and built a rancheria near Sonoita Creek that they called Fort Buchanan. Those soldiers stayed south of that trail to the setting sun and never came to this country. And four moons ago they left, too.

"Last harvest some other blue soldiers came up the San Pedro to where it meets the water of Aravaipa Creek, and there they build another fort, which they call Breckenridge. Some of those soldiers have been near the camp of Eskiminzin, and the Aravaipa bands and others have been in the country of the Pinal Apaches. These soldiers say Apaches cannot raid into Mexico any longer. Sometimes they chase raiding parties, and some livestock has been lost to them. Those soldiers are still there at that place on the Gila.

"We don't know what the soldiers are doing here, but they have many guns and wagons that they fire too. They have many horses and mules and saddles, and every day those soldiers practice shooting and never run out of ammunition. You know what those Chiricahua men told us about the soldiers trying to capture Cochise and about the big battle at Apache Pass. Many Apaches died there. Many, many white men have been killed on their trail since then, yet still there are more blue soldiers. Why they are here is what we must find out.

"So we need to be careful. You men who raid, avoid those soldiers. When you bring those cattle and horses back, stay high up in the Galiuro Mountains and cross the Aravaipa a good safe distance from the Gila. If you see those soldiers, don't bring them back to this camp because that could be bad for us if they found out where we live. You boys who keep watch here, always keep a sharp eye out for any smoke or dust or anything shiny, for it might be blue soldiers. You women there, store some of this food where we can have it in case we have to move so the people won't go hungry. Now, let's all go to work!"

The people went back to their work with a somber mien. This had been a big talk for Long Ears. He must have been thinking about this for a long time. Maybe he was right. What were these white men doing here? Where did they come from? Why don't they leave like the others?

As he walked back to his *gowa*, Nakaidoklinni stopped to watch two lizards at play, and he saw that their skin had a different cast from any he had seen before.

· · · · · · · · · · · ·

The cold moons passed without incident, and the round of life continued much as before. Nakaidoklinni passed his time by learning all the plant lore that he could. He was slowly becoming a respected medicine man as his understanding of healing ceremonials and herbal remedies expanded. Whenever he was called upon to minister to the people, he always sang his wolf songs, sometimes to himself before he left his *gowa* and sometimes during the curing rite. He always had a small medicine bag with him in which he kept a sliver of the lightning wood he had found, along with some bits of turquoise, some wolf fur, the tip of a tail feather of an eagle, and a small, black, finely wrought arrow point that he had found one day while helping Ilnaba in the cornfield. Any time that he was asked to help someone who was sick or hurt, if he didn't know what to do he would build up a fire until the coals were glowing and he would peer deep inside searching for that wolf, and sometimes he saw him and sometimes not. But always that wolf led him and helped him as long as he had surrendered his will and opened his being. Often after a cure, Nakaidoklinni would go off and purify himself in a sojourn of solitary meditation, and as time passed, these periods grew longer in duration. There were different places that he would go, depending on how he felt or what his concerns were, and in each place he could build a sweat lodge and exist for days on roots or berries or nuts, maybe bringing a pouch of piñole and always a bag of sacred *hoddentin*, the yellow pollen of purification.

Thus the moons waxed and waned, the seasons revolved in the heavens, the leaves turned from green to red to brown and back to green again. During the harvest after Long Ears' warning to the people, it was said that the soldiers had built another fort at the place where they had attempted to capture Cochise. The harvest after that one, it was said that Mangas Coloradas has been captured and killed, his head cut off and taken, while his body was thrown into a gully. Three harvests from that time, when Tulan, Nakaidoklinni and Ilnaba's son, was born, the sands, rocks, and mountains of Apacheria had all been stirred by a giant hand until all was muddy and nothing was clear as it had been long, long ago. Now there was Fort Goodwin, Fort Whipple, Fort Lowell, Fort Verde, Fort McDowell, Fort Tubac, Fort Thomas, and there was no end to the soldiers. Everywhere a new fort appeared, more round wagons came with white men who built houses, broke the land, raised cattle, or mined the white and yellow metals. Every day Apacheria was more tightly ringed than the last. Every day brought more incursions to the land of the *Nde*. Every moon, more braves, more women would be killed.

Every spring a new crop of uncertainty, of impermanence was planted, and every fall the large bitter fruit ripened even when no other crops did so.

In Tulan's first two years, the Apache people were like hornets when their nest is disturbed, and anyone who crossed their path was stung. Every moon, regardless of the season, groups of warriors would gather their weapons, paint their bodies, and prepare to strike the white man. If a warrior was killed on a raid, then another raid would be formed to avenge him on the white men. Sometimes they raided along the Gila, other times along the wagon trail west. The San Pedro was hit so often that nearly all of its ranches had been abandoned and there were few settlers left in that direction. And still the white men came.

It was at this time that a Coyotero warrior from the camp of Diablo came to see Long Ears, and that night it was passed that a large ceremony was to take place in one moon in the camp of Diablo. All of the people of Long Ears' band looked forward to this time and began to prepare by getting food ready, looking to their moccasins, checking their saddles, and seeing that their finery was in good repair. And so in the time of Many Leaves the people journeyed to that place of Diablo's. Although many Coyotero people were there when they arrived, Long Ears' people were able to set up camp on Ash Flat, which was known to all for its fine-flavored acorns.

Many camps had decided to meet here, and not all of the groups were traditionally friendly, so Long Ears was wary and cautioned all of the people to be on their best behavior. Some Pinal Apaches were in attendance, and some others from the San Pedro and Aravaipa under their leaders Eskiminzin and Captain Chiquito. Miguel was there with his band, and so was

Pedro and his people. There were some Chiricahuas with Cochise and even some Warm Springs people. That evening a huge bonfire was lit and a dance of welcome was held for all of the guests. Some of Miguel's group had brought large *tusses* filled with *tiswin*, but few got drunk because there were so many people at the dance. Yet it went on till nearly dawn, when finally the last dog went back to his camp as the sun was poking over the hills to the east.

That night the purpose of the meeting was revealed as Diablo addressed the people after all had their fill of the mule and venison that had been cooked for the large gathering.

"My brothers and sisters," he said. "Child of the Waters and White Painted Woman gave this land to the *Nde* long, long ago. The old ones say that it has been ours before time and that before the sands were made the people who were in this place hunted deer and grew corn. These mountains and valleys have been where we have lived, and our spirits walk the land and live in the rocks and streams. We know that this is so." Nakaidoklinni nodded his head and heard murmurs of agreement from those around him.

"My father said to me when I was a boy that he had been shown how to raid in Mexico and that is how he got to be a warrior with a strong heart. And his father before him became a man in Mexico and learned to stand up to them and fight because they told him, 'Don't get scared and run off.' And that is how the *nancin* were kept from this land that has been given to us.

"Now come these white men, these blue soldiers. First, they too fought the Mexican, so some of the people said maybe they were going to be on our side. Some people said they only want the yellow metal and that is why they go toward the setting sun. But now they stay here, and every harvest sees more blue soldiers, more wagons, more guns, and more dead Apaches. We have fought them just like the *nancin*. Our lances and bullets pierce them and they bleed and die, but more come and find our rancherias, burn our corn and wickiups, destroy our caches so we have to live like animals and freeze through the winter. I have a weak heart when we fight the white man, and my head is no good for this."

The crowd was silent now, and Nakaidoklinni could see that all eyes were on Diablo, each person carefully weighing his words and anticipating where he was going and what he would say next.

"Too many ranchers and miners want our lands. When white men come, they stay and build their casa, and maybe another white man comes then and builds another one, and every time this happens the Apaches lose more hunting land, more places where we have farmed.

"Two moons ago a white *nantan* came to this place for a big talk. He said his heart was heavy that the Apache and the white man fight all the time and that white farmers take our land. He spoke that the land is big enough for both to live side by side in peace. He said the blue soldiers would keep the white settlers out of our land if we give them some place to build a fort."

"This I am doing because my heart is weak and my head is no good for this. They can put a fort there on the Rio Blanco and maybe we will live in peace."

At this, Diablo sat down to the stunned silence of the people. Only the songs of birds stirred the air, and overhead a hawk wheeled around the sun, shattering the day with his piercing whistle. And then

Loco stood and faced the people. Loco was a powerfully built man with broad shoulders and deep chest. His face was strong with clean lines but sleepy eyes and his hair was swept back and tied with a white headband. A blue tunic, open at the throat, exposed a necklace of beads with a rounded leather five-pointed star affixed to it. His breechcloth was worn over white pants that were tucked into his high-topped moccasins. Loco was known to be a wise leader and had many followers.

"The Warm Springs people have known the white man for nearly thirty harvests. After the war with Mexico they came to mark the boundary and stayed with us for many moons. They came in peace and there were not many blue soldiers, but they did take some Mexicans that belonged to our people. But they promised they would leave, and they did as they said.

"Then miners came to dig in the earth, and these men stayed. Sometimes they would shoot at our warriors if the party was small so we would take their horses and mules, but those men stayed. Blue soldiers came to get the horses, but we would escape to the hills and kill the horses if we were followed too closely.

"My heart is also heavy because they keep us from Ojo Caliente, where our ancestors lived. My heart is heavy because they killed our leader Mangas Coloradas and took his head so that his ghost is restless. Why did they take his head?

"Many forts have been built where we used to roam, and blue soldiers have come back in great numbers after they left to fight the gray soldiers. At first our people thought that we had driven them from our lands, but we were wrong. It did not work right for us.

"We can go to the Sierra Madre in Mexico and live the old way and only have to fight the Mexican soldiers, but my heart is in Ojo Caliente and the mountains of the fathers. If peace can be made with the white man, if we can stay in our land, it would be good."

After this was said, Cochise spoke too, in favor of peace if his band could stay in the Chiricahuas and not have white men encroach on their lands or their way of life. Some men from the Pinalinos got up after that and said that the soldiers could not fight in their mountains and that they would keep the miners from trespassing just as their fathers had kept the Mexicans and the Spaniards from digging in the earth. Other men from the Tonto stood up and said much the same thing, that their country was too rough for white men, and that they were able to raid at will and ambush any attempts at retaliation. They said that if Diablo wanted a fort and white men in his fathers' lands, that was all right for him and his people, but that their people would still be at war with all of the whites and would be until the stones melted beneath their feet.

Now Long Ears stood, and Nakaidoklinni watched him closely but was unable to guess where he stood or what he would say.

"My brothers, when we were asked to this place we did not know why we were coming. They just said that there was to be a meeting and a dance like our people have. When we rode over here, we went as we always go and the trails went the same, along the Rio Blanco with the same trees and the same hills. The yellow flowers still stood and the vines are red like always in this season. The water still flows downhill and the acorns are still sweet here at this place. But my brothers, the sands have shifted, and who can say that the mountains will still be here tomorrow or that the sun will rise as it has in the past. We can feel the difference in the morning breeze and life is not as it once was.

"Once we let the wind blow us across this land where it wished to carry us, and wherever we were it was good. Now when the wind blows, we hide behind a boulder or hold a big tree, and if we let go, who knows where we end up or if we will ever find the way back to our homes. Can we ever be free again to do as we wish? Who in his heart believes that the white man will ever leave or that we can turn him back and live again like the ancients?"
· · · · · · · · · · · · ·

And so the band of Long Ears broke camp and trailed back to the valley where their wickiups stood among the junipers, above the cottonwoods that grew along the stream that watered their fields. Each person knew in his heart that the old ways were gone and that every member would have to get up each morning and pick a path through the day in deliberation, in consideration of new powers and new gods that would be revealed to them. If they were lucky, maybe they would choose the good path.

Nakaidoklinni rode in front of Ilnaba and his son. What does this all mean, he wondered. Silently, giving the pony his head, Nakaidoklinni strained to hear the heartbeat of the land, but all there was were the echoes of the past. Out of the corner of his eye he watched for the shadow of a white wolf slinking in the trees. His only reward was an occasional squirrel or perhaps a falling leaf. Years after, he looked back on this day as the watershed of his life, but he already knew this in his heart as he rode that pony home.

Again and again means were adopted and put into execution for the suppression of inroads and incursions of the Apache. . . . Men and adventurers having nothing in particular to do, would frequently follow them for a week at a time and nearly always fail to find them and return after they were half worn out, disgusted with their efforts. . . . The greatest science in fighting these Indians was the art of finding them at all and then catching them off their guard.

Daniel Ellis Connor,
Joseph Reddeford Walker and the Arizona Adventure

For the next six days after the return to camp, Nakai-doklinni considered the words of Diablo and the other leaders, often discussing them with Sanchez. A fort on the Rio Blanco would mean that they would see soldiers all the time and that the places they lived would be known to the white men.

"This cannot be good for the people," muttered Sanchez. "My heart is hard. I don't tremble and run before the bullets of the white man.

"Let us live as we always have. We are not turkeys tied to trees. We are not birds in cages of twigs."

"This is so," agreed Nakaidoklinni. "Our people have always been free as the wolf and the coyote. But a wolf can be trapped, and a coyote can be taken from its den and tamed. Diablo wants to make a big cage, not to keep us in but to keep the white men out."

"It is the Apache who has kept the Mexican in the cage."

"True. But they don't have so many soldiers. Not every Mexican has a pistol, a rifle, and a knife."

"Yes, and the white man knows how to shoot straight. But so do we."

· · · · · · · · · · · · ·

That night Nakaidoklinni had a dream in which he saw himself standing in front of a white man. He wore his shaman's shirt with the medicine cord, and around him whirled his *tzi-ditindi,* roaring out the name of Monster Slayer, summoning powers from deep within the earth. The white man raised his rifle, taking deliberate aim at the shaman, and shot three times, but each time the bullet hit the shirt and fell at Nakaidoklinni's feet, until in disgust the white man mounted his horse and rode away.

Now Nakaidoklinni felt himself get tall, stretching skyward until he looked down at his feet and they appeared like tiny ants. As he looked down, a storm cloud blew up from behind his shoulder and moved down a wide valley to a place where there was a bluff with white rocks at the top. Tremendous, blinding bolts of lightning were hurled repeatedly until the white rocks were loosened into an avalanche careening down the slope. In the morning he told Ilnaba that he would be going for some days to White Rocks Fall Down to talk with the old man, Nasta.

· · · · · · · · · · · · ·

The eyes of the ancient shaman stared at Nakaidoklinni without expression. He lived in perpetual darkness now, in a small wickiup near that of his sister's girl, and it was she who looked after him.

"It would be good to make a fire to heat rocks for

a sweat," Nasta suggested. "After we purify ourselves we can talk."

A small sweat lodge was behind the old man's wick-

iup, and there was already a stack of wood near a pit and a small pile of rocks. The sweat lodge was as high as Nakaidoklinni's chest and round so that a man could nearly stretch out flat inside. It was built with an oak frame and thatched with brush. A cowhide was draped over the top. There was a small, east-facing entry, and just inside to the right was a depression to hold the stones.

As the fire burned down and the rocks were heated, both men stripped down to loincloths. Nasta felt around at the base of the lodge until he grasped a bowl of crushed piñon needles, and this he rubbed over himself and then Nakaidoklinni did the same. Next, both men tied sage around their heads. Nakaidoklinni, using forked sticks, moved the stones to the pit inside, and both entered, Nasta last, pulling a hide over the opening of the door.

As Nasta sprinkled water on the hot rocks, a sizzle and a pop was heard and the steam began filling the small space. Nakaidoklinni breathed deeply, feeling steam on his forehead and neck, smelling the fragrance of piñon needles, and then the old man began singing. He sang about the sweat bath, the sky and the earth, singing the same songs over again in turn.

The young shaman heard the words of the old man's songs and felt them work into his pores along with the steam. The gentle rivers of sweat running off his forehead and shoulders lulled him and pulled him back to the earth from which all comes. He could hear the blood drum in his body, keeping cadence with Nasta's songs. Time and thought were suspended. The sweat lodge was neither of the earth nor the sky, but a nether place, subject to its own laws, customs, and history.

Nasta chanted prayers to his own powers, and there were refrains that Nakaidoklinni chanted with him. Each time a song was finished, more water was sprinkled on the stones until finally they produced no more steam. One more song of thanks was given, the hide was thrown back, and the men followed the path down to the stream, where Nakaidoklinni found a deep hole to immerse himself in while Nasta sat by the edge of the water and splashed himself.

"Now we can make words," smiled Nasta. "They say that the blue soldiers are building a fort on the Rio Blanco."

"Why," thought Nakaidoklinni, "do I think that I'm going to tell the old medicine man anything new?" He proceeded to tell about the meeting he had attended and about the soldiers that were on the Rio Blanco. Then they talked about the old days when Nasta was young, before there were white men in the Apache land. Nasta related in great detail the story of the first raid he made to Mexico. On this raid he saw a pueblo that was the town of Fronteras, with its plaza, large white church, and thick-walled adobe buildings. This was when he first realized that not everyone lived like the People.

"I said to myself, maybe because these people live in a casa and make a big white wickiup, maybe they are different. Maybe these arrows don't go through them. Maybe they can run like the small deer with the white tail. Maybe these people don't die when their blood makes the sand red.

"Then our men went right up and caught their

horses, right in the daytime when they could see us. The Mexicans stayed within the walls with the doors shut. So we rode right into that place, up and down each street, and then right into the big white house. No one came to stop us, so we left with our herd.

"Then those *nancin* came out and some still had horses, so our men let them catch up. We killed them and took those horses, too. Those Mexicans died just like everything else. Their pueblos and casas meant nothing.

"Mexicans and white men and Apaches all die because of Coyote. One time Coyote picked up a rock and this is what he said: 'I am going to throw this rock into some water I know about, and if this rock floats, people will live forever. If this rock sinks, then all the people will have to die, just like all the other animals.' So that is what happened. Coyote threw the rock high up in the sky. It kept going up there till it was so small you couldn't see it. Everyone looked to the four directions and straight up, but it had disappeared. Then hawk said, 'I see it.' Then Bear said, 'I see it.' Then everyone saw it, and they said they could hear it too! Here it came, getting bigger and bigger, going faster and faster. Suddenly it hit that water and went straight in so you couldn't see it anymore, and Coyote said that the rock didn't float. That's why we all have to die. That's why anyone can be killed, even a white man or a Mexican. It doesn't matter who you are.

"The young people, all the time they come and ask me, 'Why do we have to have Mexicans and white men?' This is what they say.

"First there was White Painted Woman, who has always been, and then there was Killer of Enemies. One time White Painted Woman got by Water and then she had a boy named Child of the Water. This boy grew really fast, and he and Killer of Enemies started hunting together for some monsters that were here back then. There were giant eagles, and antelope that could just look at you and you would die. There were dangerous buffalo, too, and all of these had to be beaten and conquered. Then they had to agree to be useful for the People, and that is how we got birds, from those eagle feathers.

"Most of these animals that we have here now were kept under the ground in an animal home that Killer of Enemies found out about. So he let them out to roam around.

"Now this place was ready for people. Child of the Water got some clouds, and this is what he did next: first he made Apaches, and then he made the white men. There were plenty of each one, but he had to tell them what to do because they didn't know anything. So Child of the Waters picked some things for the Apaches. He got them bows and arrows, and all the wild food, and the mountains with the forests. Killer of Enemies chose for the white men. They got guns, and they got seeds that could be planted. And they got land where they could plant crops, raise cattle, and dig the shiny metal.

"This is why we have white men. This is why they are coming to the Rio Blanco."

· · · · · · · · · · · · ·

The next day, Nakaidoklinni told about the dream he had telling him to come to White Rocks Fall Down. Nasta asked him to describe the shirt he was wearing then.

"It was the shirt of a *diyi*. It was the shirt that was made here in this place White Rocks Fall Down. It had symbols for lightning and the white wolf. There was a pointed moon, the sun, and rain. There was snake, tarantula, and centipede. This is the shirt I wear when someone comes to ask for the *izze-nantan*. This is the shirt I wear with the sash, my hat, and medicine cord."

"Perhaps there was something on that shirt that had not been there before?"

Nakaidoklinni thought for a long time.

"There was something new. There was a man walking on a cloud and there was a yellow cross. These I had not seen before."

"These visions are not always easy to understand. Keep looking for a man on a cloud and for the yellow cross. Yellow is the color of the sacred pollen, *hodden-tin*. The rest you will have to find out. You dreamed this when a white man was in your dream and his bullets fell to the ground. Walking on a cloud, a yellow cross, and the white man. These all are together in there. You will have to find what they mean."

· · · · · · · · · · · · ·

Nakaidoklinni returned to his wickiup, his heart full now that he had been with Nasta. That night, as he played with Tulan, his doubts and worries receded to the shadows. His boy was full of laughter, and though he was small, he was strong and quick. Nakaidoklinni enjoyed his son and would like to have more, but so far Ilnaba had birthed only one child.

*I don't want to run over the mountains any more; I want to make
a big treaty. . . . I will keep my word until the stones melt. . . . I
will put a rock down to show that when it melts the treaty will be
broken. . . . I promise that when a treaty is made the white man
or soldiers can turn out all their horses and mules without any
one to look after them, and if they are stolen by the Apaches I will
cut my throat.*

Delshay to Capt. Netterville,
from Dan L. Thrapp, *The Conquest of Apacheria*

In three moons, in the time of Large Leaves, the first
soldiers came to the Rio Blanco. Smoke from signal
fires told of their coming as all around the telltale
puffs filled the blue sky. They were not the smokes
of alarm or flight, but merely told of the passings and
the progress of the soldiers. Many people followed
the smoke and then went to the forks of the Rio
Blanco to see the blue intruders there where they
had established camp. Nakaidoklinni and Sanchez
were among the group who rode from Long Ears'
camp on the Carrizo, each man riding his finest
mount. Each warrior carried his weapons, and many
wore painted faces for this occasion, though the paint
was not the paint of the warpath.

Other parties were also going to see the white men,
many traveling up the trail along the Rio Blanco.
When the river's forks came into sight Nakaidoklinni
could see the white tents of the soldiers across the river

and a large group of Apaches on the other side, some mounted and others on foot or simply sitting and watching what was happening.

There were more than a hundred of the blue soldiers. They had a large herd of horses and mules, and pickets were set out, guns to the ready, keeping the Apaches across the river. Nakaidoklinni watched as some boys crossed the water in the direction of the horses. A soldier quickly approached and motioned for them to go back. It seemed that the first Apache word all the soldiers learned was *u-ka-she,* which means "go away."

All the soldiers first appeared to be dressed the same, but upon closer inspection there was variation. Most soldiers had just the blue clothes, but a few had pants of a different kind, including some made of rawhide. Some soldiers had bare heads and others had blue soldier hats. Many wore black hats with high crowns. Several had bandannas around their necks, and every man had a pistol belt and knife and often another belt for ammunition. Some wore long swords at their sides like those the Apaches would take from dead Mexican soldiers to make their lances. Most were garbed in long-sleeved blue shirts or blue coats with shiny buttons. This clothing seemed to be the major point of discussion among many of the people. And, of course, everyone argued the relative merits of the various horses and mules.

Now a white man not dressed in blue rode to the river, crossed, and got Diablo and Pedro to return with him for a talk with the chief of the soldiers. They rode into the soldier camp, each man keeping his weapons. When they dismounted the people could see them being introduced to four different soldiers who all had full blue uniforms.

There was a festive air about the crowd, and its ranks continued swelling as more people arrived. Every time someone attempted to cross the stream he was warned back. Those who had arrived early had become the experts on the white men by virtue of their hours of advantage over any latecomers, and they were quick to point out anything that seemed worth remarking about. Finally Diablo and Pedro returned and addressed the people, saying that these soldiers were from Camp Grant and that they were here to choose a site for a fort and to select a route for a road for the wagons that soldiers use. Diablo said that the People were to stay out of the camp and to keep on the opposite side of the river. The *nantan* captain who spoke for the soldiers had warned that the guards would be posted at all times and that anyone who tried to enter the camp without permission would be shot. He had asked Pedro if any of the Apaches on the other side of the river were hostile. Pedro replied that they were all Coyoteros and that none were on the warpath. The *nantan* said that any camps that harbored hostiles would be attacked and that the soldiers would burn fields or wickiups of Apaches who were not friendly, but that the soldiers came in peace and wanted to live as brothers.
· · · · · · · · · · · · ·

From this time on, there were soldiers at that place. First it was named Camp Ord, and later Camp Mogollon. Then the name was changed to Camp Thomas and again to Camp Apache. Every time Nakaidoklinni came to the fort, it had a new name, and it made him think the white man was not one to make up his mind and stick to it.

A road was built from Camp Apache to Zuni, and

this connected with other forts in New Mexico. Another was built connecting Camp Apache to Camp Goodwin, and when this was complete, wagons were able to bring in supplies and the soldiers started building the fort. They cut many trees to make the walls of their buildings. When the building was complete, the soldiers held a fiesta with beef butchered for all of the people who attended, both Apache and white. A blue soldier general came to the fiesta to make a talk. He said that his government had made a place for the Apaches and that was why this fort was here. From now on the Apaches would have the land that would run from the Mogollon Rim south through Sombrero Butte to the highest peaks in the Gila Mountains. It would go east from there to the boundary of New Mexico and then north to a line even again with the Mogollon Rim. This, the general soldier said, would be Indian land, and the white man would have to go somewhere else. He also said that the Apaches could not raid anymore, and because of this the soldiers would have beef to kill for the People. Someone asked if he would give some horses or mules instead, but he said it would only be cattle.

As this blue general talked, Nakaidoklinni felt the stones shift under his feet. The old ways were gone. Now the People would be given meat instead of making their own by going to Mexico. Now there was a place called Apache land with invisible lines on the ground. Here was Apache land but one more step might not be. Thus the warrior was penned up like a horse in a corral, and maybe the white man would have to stay out of the pen, but the Apache had always been free to go where his feet took him and this was no longer so.

Each person there knew the old ways were gone. How would they live now? How could they call themselves Apaches if they were not to raid in Mexico? How could a boy become a man? Where would a man win horses and goods to pay for a wife? Where would a family get all the gifts to give for the puberty ceremony of their daughters? How could the old stories of long, long ago guide them now? These had been as the north star to the People, always pointing the way. What would lead them now? Many questions were in the heads of the People, and each person felt as a grain of sand in a whirlwind. Each person felt he had no power of his own but must blow where the wind of the blue soldier took him.

The blue general spoke his words, and these were translated to Spanish by a different white man, who was a scout for the soldiers. This man spoke to He Who Runs, the boy Coyote Waits brought back from Mexico, the boy who had grown up to be a warrior. He Who Runs heard the words he knew from long ago and then gave the words of the blue general to the People.

"The Great White Father sends his greetings to the Apache brothers and sisters. From this day on let all men live in peace. Let the Apache stop killing white men and stealing his horses and cattle. Let the white man stop killing Apaches and burning their fields. From this day forward, let everyone know that this land is for the Apache and that it is closed to white settlement. Let the miner and his burro look somewhere else for the yellow metal. Let the farmer with his plow find other land to break.

"The Great White Father asks that all Apaches live in peace with him. Not just the Coyoteros, but all Apaches. Let the people with Cochise seek peace with their white brothers and the people of Ojo Caliente. Let the people in the Pinal Mountains lay down their bow and arrow and build their wickiups without fear of discovery. Let the people of the Tonto live in peace and gather food that will not be destroyed by the soldiers who hunt them.

"The Great White Father asks that you Coyotero people help your brothers and sisters in other bands to see the wisdom of your actions, of the peace that you have made, because the Apaches will not be safe from all white men until the last brave sees the wisdom of turning his arrow and his bullet away from his white brothers.

"Many white men say that all Apaches look alike and that all should be killed, that only then can white men be safe from fear of raiding and killing. The Great White Father does not say this and has sent his soldiers to protect the peaceful Coyoteros who live with their wise leaders like Diablo, like Pedro, like Miguel, like Long Ears, like Captain Chiquito."

Now there were many questions asked of the blue general.

Pedro stood up first. "Our people have always hunted deer and always gathered mescal. Some people say that this will not be anymore. What does the blue general say?"

"I say this to those people. The Great White Father cannot allow the warrior to go to Mexico because we agreed with that government that this would be so when this land was bought from the Mexicans. But many deer and much mescal grow here in these mountains, and it is here for the Apaches just like before."

Captain Chiquito asked, "During the time Thick with Fruit, the people have gone south to the desert to gather the red fruit of the tall cactus. We like to eat this fruit because it is sweet and this we would still do."

"If the people wish to go north to get pine nuts or west to get mescal, or south to get cactus fruit, that is fine with the Great White Father, as long as the people stay in the land he has made for the Apache people. If you want to go past the line that is on this paper, permission can be given by the commander of Fort Apache or by the agent. If you do go to get the fruit beyond the line on this paper, you will need a paper with you to show to other soldiers and white men so they will know that you have permission and are not hostiles who should be fought."

Now Diablo asked this: "Some people want to know how they will get beef from the soldiers. Some people want to know if it will be alive or already shot. Some people want to know who will get the hide."

"The beef will already be killed. The agent will know the names of all the people who are at peace and who should get meat. Every day he will have one and a half pounds of beef for every man, woman, and child. The hides will be given to the band chief and he will decide which people need moccasins or rope or hide for their wickiup."

"We do not understand what this is," said Diablo. "How can we know what a pound is?"

He Who Runs said this to the scout with the buckskin pants and he said this to the blue general. Then the blue general spoke to many white men in a group for some time. At last he said, "A pound is how heavy something is." He picked up a rock and hefted it in his hand, letting it fall to his other hand. "Say to the people that a pound is four yucca fruit."

Now Long Ears walked to the front and addressed the general.

"I have heard that the Great White Father wants to live in peace with the Coyoteros but that white men say all Apaches look alike. Yet each of our warriors answers only for himself and to his own powers. A chief leads by showing the way and by the power of his words, but each man must do as he thinks best.

"Though we speak the same tongue, each band of the People speaks for itself, and we have no government like the white man or the Mexican. A peace cannot be made by one chief for all Apaches. Not all Apaches are at all times at peace with each other. How are we to know that the peaceful people will not be taken for hostiles? How are we to know that all blue soldiers will not shoot our warriors and our women?"

"These are good words that Long Ears says," agreed the general. "These soldiers at Fort Apache who are of the First Cavalry will know where your villages are and which bands are our friends, but there are soldiers from other forts who will not know this. For this reason the Great White Father wants to give these pieces of paper with his words on them saying that each of your bands is at peace. Keep these papers with you and show them when you see soldiers who you do not know." Saying this, he called out each band chief and gave him a piece of paper with the words of the Great White Father on them. Only a few Apache had ever seen words written and most did not understand how these could be the words of anyone, but the papers were taken anyway, though no one could read them. Long Ears showed his to He Who Runs, who had seen words written when he was a boy, but the marks on the paper were indecipherable to him.

The sun had passed from the zenith until it was an orange ball in the western sky before the last question was answered. Finally the general gave out black campaign hats to the chiefs and shook their hands, and the people departed for their camps.

Nakaidoklinni and Sanchez rode together. Sanchez felt anger in his heart because the fort was now in Apache land. He did not need the white man's meat, nor the white man's paper. He could not see that the spirits of the land would smile on the People while the land was defiled by the *nancin*.

Nakaidoklinni, the more pragmatic of the two, said, "If an arm is broken, it must be set with slats split from the sotol. If an old one dies in a wickiup, it must be burned and another built in a different place. If someone was taken with owl sickness, a shaman could be called to drive the owl away. If the white man came to Apache land, perhaps something could be done to ease the pain and heal the spirit of the people." He knew, though, that it was not enough to wish the white man would go away. If there were no medicine, there could be no cure.

After returning to their wickiup, Ilnaba and her family talked about the soldiers as they chewed their mescal and jerky. Though Apache women had their duties, and work was split along the line of the sexes, this did not mean that women were not important or that they had no opinions. Many roles in the life of the People could be filled by either man or woman, and a woman could be a warrior as well as a person with the power to cure and heal. Many women did have powers of their own and were called upon by all when the need arose.

Ilnaba felt her husband's perplexity and understood why he went off for days at a time to fast on the mountain, to seek his vision. She, too, was perplexed and stirred by the events of recent times. Was there nothing that could be depended upon to be as it once was?

"My husband, when I first saw those blue soldiers, when the signal fires followed them to the Rio Blanco, it was as though I was looking through a hollow log into another world. The river was like fog between me and that place, and I could not crawl through the log or go around it either.

"Today I felt that the fog had lifted and now I could go to that place where the blue soldiers lived, but when I got there they were giants, with giant knives and guns and even giant horses. And the giants said, 'You, Little Sister, you we will keep and feed and take care of, but you must never bite us on the hand or you will feel the sting of our weapons and know the wrath of our revenge.'

"What can we do, my husband? Are we like the ants that always look before and behind so that no bear will blindly stumble along and grind them to dust? Will your son, Tulan, have to learn to live like the ant, always looking over his shoulder to see where the big animal steps, never looking forward to see where he is going? I cannot see what tomorrow will bring to our people."

11

Whitman reported that a hundred and twenty-five Apache were slain in the Camp Grant Massacre. Oury openly boasted that "about one hundred forty-four of the most bloodthirsty devils that ever disgraced mother earth" had been slaughtered. He did not trouble to mention that of the total murdered only eight were men. . . .

Twenty-seven children were taken alive, and turned over as booty to the Papago, who would sell them into slavery in Sonora.

John Upton Terrell,
Apache Chronicle

Ghost Face roared in like an angry she bear and settled in to stay. The snows piled one on another, the piercing winds chilling man and beast alike. With no break in the cold, food supplies were becoming exhausted, and each family began to ration what remained. Every dawn saw hunters going out for deer or smaller game. Those who were able to make it to Camp Apache reported that the beef was gone and that more would not be available until the mud was dry and government suppliers could bring in new herds.

At night, in the early darkness, the men sat around, knowing that this was the time to be raiding and that meat could be made by riding south. And some young men did go out on their own, but without the older men to lead they met with limited success.

Finally the sap began to rise, the buds of new life

gave their promise of renewal, and hope stirred in
the breast, temporarily relieving the hunger that
gnawed in the gut. The mescal had not yet begun to
swell, but it would not be long till the harvest could
begin, till the hunger could subside. And still the
hunters went out.

One such day, while the men of the *gota* were hunting, Ilnaba stepped from her wickiup drawn by a wail
of sorrow: a voice she did not recognize. Other women
were out too, all hurrying down toward the trail leading to the camp. A woman walking with a stick was
leading another who was slumped on a pony, and
Ilnaba saw that the woman in front was Dah-ita, a
woman of her clan who had gone to live with the
people of the Aravaipa. As the women ran to her, Dah-
ita stumbled and fell in a heap where she remained,
crying uncontrollably.

Ilnaba could see that both women were clothed in
rags so as to be practically naked. As Dah-ita was
helped to her feet and carried into the village, she
seemed to be a mass of scratches and scabs. Her feet
were bare and bled freely. Both women were led to
Ilnaba's wickiup and brought inside, being placed on
beds of skins, Dah-ita still unable to speak. One
woman went to bring some warm broth while Ilnaba
began to examine the woman who had been tied to
the horse.

This woman she did not know. As best she could
tell she was of Ilnaba's age, though the woman was
very thin, with her skin stretched tight over the bones
of her face, giving her an angular, older appearance.
There were lice in the woman's hair, and in one spot
her scalp was freshly scabbed over where hair should
have been. Dried blood caked the little clothing that
she wore, and as this was removed, Ilnaba could see

that the woman had been shot through the thigh and again through the back. As Ilnaba listened for the beat of this woman's heart, she knew that if life still flowed in this body, it was ebbing fast and would soon be gone. With her head to the woman's flat, hollow breasts, the heart barely echoed. All that could be done was to take her outside so she could die in peace, freeing her spirit to leave for the happy land.

By the time this was accomplished, the other woman had quieted down and was being given sips of the hot broth. Except for the scratches, she was not injured, but she also was unable to talk. Soon she passed out and didn't stir again until the next day, when her appetite returned, and then she was able to tell her story.

"We people of the Aravaipa had a hard winter with little to eat. Some old people starved to death, and women could not make milk for their babies so that many of them died also. We did not know what to do, so some old women walked to Camp Grant and told the *nantan* that they were hungry and that maybe their people would come in if there was anything to eat.

"Slowly, one wickiup at a time, people began leaving their homes and moving down to a valley near Camp Grant because someone said that the soldiers had food. This was so, and word spread so that soon many camps came in, and we were given white man food in cans and sacks and sometimes a little meat.

"Eskiminzin was our chief, and he made peace with the *nantan* named Lieutenant Whitman. Often the lieutenant would bring a wagon to our camp and have food for us to eat.

"We were about three hundred in number and the soldiers did not have enough food for everyone, so

the men had to keep hunting. A big party was organized to go higher in the hills to find the deer. All
men who were able left with Eskiminzin on that hunt.

"The men had been gone for two days. That night
I was sleeping in the wickiup with my children, and
just as the stars were beginning to disappear, I suddenly awoke and was tense and still, listening to the
night. I could hear feet running toward the wickiup,
and then everything around me exploded in a crack-
ling blaze of burning wickiups.

"All around me there were frightful screams and
terrified people. I gathered my children, pushing
them out of the door ahead of me, and then I could
hear shots but I couldn't tell where they were coming
from. Emerging from the wickiup, I could see Papago
men with clubs running among the people, striking
them down, so the children and I started to run toward the slope of the hill to the west where there
were boulders and trees to hide us.

"I had nearly cleared all of the wickiups and was
running hard when bullets started hitting the ground
around me. I could hear them ricocheting into the
dawn, and one passed right by my ear. We were being
chased by two men with clubs who were gaining on
us. I cried to my son and daughters to split and meet
at the top of the ridge, and the last thing I saw as I
disappeared into the chaparral was one of the men
clubbing my oldest daughter. She fell where he hit
her, and then he raised the club above his head and
hit down with all of his might, and I could hear her
head pop like a pumpkin. For a moment I stared in
disbelief, until another of my husband's sisters ran
up and slapped me, telling me to run for my life.

"Bullets were still whistling from every direction.
The light of the burning wickiups made it seem almost

like day, but smoke burned my eyes and brought the smell of burning flesh, of singed hair. Terrified and gasping for breath, I scrambled through the brush, finally reaching the boulder on the slope, where I slowed to get my breath.

"I kept making my way up the hill, the sounds below receding with every step. I couldn't see anyone else with me and did not dare call out, so I just kept on going and going, not sure where, just away.

"At the top of the ridge I took one look at our camp before crossing to the other side, where it would be easier to climb unobserved. The shots had died down, but the smoke was very thick. Here and there it would blow clear and everywhere I saw bodies. The Papago were going from body to body, pounding the heads flat with clubs and rocks. There were white men, too, watching the Papago, and there were many of our children on the ground there where the white men were.

"I stumbled to the other side of the ridge and climbed in silence till the sun was high. At last I could go no farther, so I climbed into some rocks to hide, not knowing what else to do.

"The shadows were getting long. The cold was seeping into my body, and my mouth was dry because there had been no water all day, and still I hid in that hole, fearful of every sound, of every shadow. I had not seen another person since daybreak.

"Suddenly a twig snapped up the slope from where I was and I melted down into the rocks as much as possible, hiding my head and being utterly still. I didn't even breathe but just listened, and there was a scraping of rock that was nearer. I knew that I, too, was going to die from the Papago war club, and I could feel the vibrations of the air as the club pushed it aside, making a path for the blow that would end my life.

"Then I could hear a soft death chant and knew that the spirits were calling me. I made ready to die when it stopped and I heard someone crying softly.

"I slowly opened my eyes and raised up, muscle by muscle, till I could see out of the rocks, and there was a wife of Eskiminzin sitting on a rock under a mesquite tree. She was the one who was crying. Softly I called to her till she knew who I was, and then I crawled down out of the rocks. She ran to me, we were there by ourselves holding each other as the sun dropped below the mountains. Then we decided to go back to the *gota* to see if we could find anyone else still alive or any food.

"It took a long time to get down off the mountain in the dark. We couldn't see where to go and didn't want to make noise in case the enemy was still there. We just kept working our way down, not sure where we would come out in the valley. Here and there we would hit deer trails and then lose them in the dark, but the slope got less steep, until we found ourselves on the valley floor below our camp. There was still the smell of smoke on the breeze, and it looked like there was a fire still burning. Cautiously, we crept up that direction, keeping to the shadows, staying in the bushes and trees.

"We knew the enemy was gone when we heard the keening for the dead, so we walked on in to the fire that had about twenty people huddled around it, and then we also saw a wagon with some soldiers and Lieutenant Whitman.

"The sun had been high when the soldiers arrived at the camp and the enemy was gone. Everywhere they looked they found people dead. They dug a big hole in the earth and buried many more than a hundred. Many more.

"The *nantan* Whitman said that white men from Tucson had done this, and that the Papago had come with them. All the children were taken by the Papago for slaves.

"We slept on the ground that night, doing whatever we could to keep warm. The soldiers had some meat and some corn, but food did not taste good to me. Even after drinking my fill, I was thirsty and tired.

"In the morning it was more than I could do to look around and see the devastation. My daughter had been buried there, and my other children were carried off by the enemy. I left word for my husband that I was going here to Long Ear's camp and started walking. In a while I found my husband's sister on the ground next to that pony. I tied her on and brought her here too."

... **12** ....

You all know that all the people can't get along very well in the world.

Words of the Apache Kid,
from Dan L. Thrapp,
Al Sieber, Chief of Scouts

In two more days, Long Ears and the hunters returned. A thunderstorm of two deer and three elk
loaded the ponies, easing the hunger of the *gota,*
breaking the drought of meat that had besieged
the people.

Daily, more word drifted in from the Aravaipa: tales
of murder, kidnapping, and atrocity, of children
hacked to death, of women raped and shot. Loose
talk in Tucson filtered back to Camp Apache soldiers.
The people cried for the return of their children.
Many had been taken to Sonora and sold to work in
mines or fields or the houses of the rich. Wild with
rage and grief, Eskiminzin took to the mountain trails
where nothing checked the blood lust of his warriors
as they purged their seared souls in the dark cold
waters of retribution.
. . . .

Ilnaba saw that her husband had a heavy heart. Many
men voiced their bitterness at the killings, the attack
being like a dead sentinel standing in the forest, at-
tracting the lightning of every cloud. Storms roiled

in every breast. Deeply buried feelings sheared loose, floating free in a bitter magma of suppressed hostilities, of dreams of what might have been, rising to the surface with gathering force until they erupted in vents of frustration, cauldrons of rage.

"The dead must be avenged."

"An Apache must stand and be a man."

"Ussen has deserted the People."

"The soul of the past, the spirits of the land are offended at the trespassing of the white man."

These words reverberated through all the wickiups wherever Apache camps were to be found.

Diablo said, "This country has always been my home and the home of my fathers. This place pleases me. I know the names of every mountain and stream. All the animals and trees are known to me. The seasons are the friends of my people. It is here where we can live with happiness and die in contentment.

"The Great White Father protects this land from the settler and the miner and protects us too, but still evil may come. We have seen the soldiers wearing ball and chain when they have broken the rules and done a bad thing. Those scorpions and centipedes who killed the Aravaipa have broken the rules. Leave this to the white man's ways for them to be punished."

Through this, Nakaidoklinni listened to one and then the other, but words did not come to his mouth. Where was the clear path? Who could be listened to so that the people could be guided and not have stones to stumble against? Where was the plain road for the people to take so they could sleep well, so fear would not howl in their ears, so hunger would not track in relentless determination? He made ready to fast and meditate in his mountains. Ilnaba saw this and was not surprised.

. . . .

The time was Many Leaves. White, puffy clouds still filled the sky, bringing the last rains before the days would turn clear, blue, and dry. The fruit grew in the progressively warm days of summer, each night shorter than the last. Nakaidoklinni walked on a westerly course, following the rising slope of the green land, working his way around arroyos and broken drainages that gave the land its distinctive character, that made it Apache country.

"I will let this valley speak to me in its many voices. All around me there is life. I will talk with the grass and the flowers, the bushes and the trees, the hawk and the robin, the deer and the bear. I will place my ear to the ground and listen to the earth and the very rocks that make the hills and mountains. Let them speak to me in their voices and I will listen."

So he listened as he walked with measured steps, respecting all that surrounded him, seeing that nothing stood on its own, that each tree was anchored in the soil and lent its branches to the birds. Yet each tree respected its kind and didn't crowd too close, didn't attack with its roots or its limbs. All was of a whole.

Seeing this as he did, it seemed natural to invite some of the wood spirits, some of the rock spirits to journey with him, to see a different place, to contemplate with him the powers that controlled all, whether visible or not. He tucked a sprig of paintbrush, a green acorn, a walnut leaf, a jay feather, and some colored stones into a bag at his waist, inviting them to a big talk on the mountain. And so he climbed, not knowing where he was going, but listening for the chorus of voices that would announce, "Stay here. You are welcome to shed your load and share the warmth of this spot. Just sit down and rest. Clear your mind and let the glory of this place wash over you, let it purify your soul."

On and on his feet led him, his slim frame effortlessly working higher. Passing through a saddle, he paused to appreciate the view before him. "There is the Rio Blanco. There is the canyon of the Rio Negro. There they join their waters to make the Rio Salado. Over there is Carrizo Canyon and the valley of the Cibique. There is the Mogollon Rim, there is the sacred mountain of the *Gan.* There lies the Gila. Beyond is the San Pedro and the Aravaipa. The Natanes Rim is at that place, and the Rio San Carlos there. Welcome to this place, son of Nak-ai-tulan." And he realized that everything around was whispering to him, bidding him to stay.

He cleared a spot of ground where all the land could be viewed, from the grasses and bushes, to the trees on nearby hills, to the blue-green in the distance that faded and folded into the sky. Around him he arranged the paintbrush and stones and all the other voices who had asked to come along. And when all were settled, they breathed deeply and exhaled, breathed deeply and exhaled, and listened with all the senses to see who else might make a presence known.

Cicada spoke up first. "I am here in this tree on the north side of this saddle." Nakaidoklinni honored Cicada with a pinch of *hoddentin.*

Then Wind blew out from behind a pile of rocks. "Over here in the west am I. I come from the desert and will carry messages to all the voices of my people." Nakaidoklinni honored this presence with another pinch of the sacred pollen. Before it could reach the ground, Wind picked it up in a gentle swirl, balancing the *hoddentin* in a high golden vortex before, with a puff, it disappeared.

Next came Ant. First this way, then that way, then back the way he had come until finally there he was. "I am Ant. Nobody notices where I go, so I hear all and see all there is to see. I go in circles so not to show a purpose, but my circles are wide and cover the earth. I am one of the under-earth people, and in my caves many voices echo, even those of the past. Let me speak for the world below."

Now the shadow of Red Tail crossed from the south. High above pierced its cascading whistle. "I am here in the blue sky high above the earth. Nothing escapes my keen eye as I ride the wind from dawn to dark. I will speak for all the people of the clouds, even Lightning and Rainbow."

"Zinn, zinn; zinn, zinn." Here was Hummingbird standing in the air on green wings. "Every year I follow the flowers north and then return to the south where I live. I have seen many things in my seasons that few have ever learned of. There are beautiful flowers beyond imagination and trees made of butterfly wings. I speak for all those voices from the south."

The day was long now. Shadows swooped low, catching the earth in their folds, muffling the sounds of the day. Everyone sat there, breathing in, breathing out. The warm air from the valleys below permeated all, bathing everything with a fine-scented fragrance drawn from all the blossoms of the desert.

Last to speak was Nakaidoklinni. "I, the son of Nak-ai-tulan, come from the east. I am of the Apache people, who were put in this place by White Painted Woman. We drink from its waters and eat of its fruits and meats. Our houses we make of sticks and skins and grasses. All that we have and need is provided by the animal people and the green things that live here."

And then he sang,

I have come to this place
to hear the spirits of the land.
I have come to this place
to hear the spirits of my people.

This he sang four times, and then he listened. He listened for that night and its day and the next night and its day and for the night and day that followed.

His body could be seen sitting there. But he was not just of the body. He had become that place on that saddle, high up the valley, overlooking the hills, across from the mountains. His eyes were the eyes of that place, his ears were the ears of that place. His being, his presence, looked down, across, and up from every tree, every rock, every ant, every sprig of paintbrush, every acorn. And many voices spoke through those ears.

One said, "The waters always flow down the stream. Now they are deep and fast, now again they are slow and warm. Rocks tumble down through the water, trees fall in its deep pools, but still the Water people remain. They do not climb out and live on the land."

Another said, "You, son of Nak-ai-tulan, are you a warrior or a healer? Which do your people need now?"

Another came and said, "Be like Coyote. Coyote is bigger and faster than Rabbit people and eats Rabbit whenever he can. Coyote is smaller than Apache people and slower than their arrows, so Coyote digs a hole when they are near."

Another said, "The Ant people live in holes all the time. We bring our food there to have it through the winter. There we have our eggs and hatch our young. When Elk people walk on our house, their hooves sink in and mash us without a thought. When they are gone, we make more tunnels and lay more eggs."

Another said, "See the Acorn people. Their numbers on the trees are without measure. Some grow fat and full, but some Wasp stings and these are hollow. All fall under the tree. Then Squirrel comes, and Jay and Turkey. They eat all the acorns they can find. But are there still not oak trees? Will there be no acorns in the spring?"

And now it was the fourth night and still everyone stayed at the big talk. Darker, darker grew the night. Fainter, fainter grew the shadows. The hard dark edge of all got harder as the sky glowed from the stars in the firmament. Owl was there and Nighthawk. Deer came by, and Skunk. All were quiet and listened to the darkness, to the thin shadows that lurk behind every rock and tree.

The eyes of Nakaidoklinni saw the wheeling stars over the saddle in their nightly rounds, yet they too kept their expectant silence. They too listened through his ears.

And there in the distance they heard the low chanting that sometimes the night makes, a shadow song for shadow ears. From every ant hole, every coyote burrow, every nest of the dirt bee, wafted the shadowy *thump-thump* of hard stick on tight cowhide. A quivering *thump-thump* from the mighty breast of Earth Mother. Folded in the blackness of night, this old white-haired chanting, dark and ghostlike to the ears, brighter and harder to the holes in the skin. Subtle but deeper in the bone. The son of Nak-ai-tulan heard this in his flesh, heard its rainbow radiance in his chest, felt the ancient sound flow back to the earth, holding him there like a rock on a mountain. Almost everyone was here at the big talk.

> Old Wolf, I'm hunting you.
> I call you now, to this saddle.
> You gave me power
> to call you here.

Back and forth came this wolf call, this earth thump, these shadow chants, these ant hole songs, and another wolf call.

> Old White One, I'm hunting you.
> I call you now, to this place.
> You gave me power
> to call you here.

From some folded place, not far off, came a deep throaty howl timbering and calling in the bone, in the hair, in the feet, inching and coming closer by each thump, each white-haired chant.

> Old Wolf, I'm hunting you.
> We call you now, to this saddle.
> You gave me power
> to call you here.

Through a rip in the darkness, another howl painted the night, higher on the hill now, closer than before, blending in the *thump-thump*, hiding in the chanting, howling again into the earth, the mournful wolf talk coming now from below all that was.

Old White One, I'm hunting you.
I call you now, to this place.
You gave me power
to call you here.

. . .

The son of Nak-ai-tulan reached for his medicine bag
and, taking out the white fur he had from long ago,
placed the fur across from where he protruded from
the earth. A wailing, labored howl blew the wind,
shook every leaf, pierced every hole, even the folds
of the night. And when its echoes had reverberated
from each rock and filled the night so it would hold
no more, the white wolf took form from the shadows
just where the white fur summoned.

The wolf was thin, with bony haunches, yellow
teeth, and yellow eyes. "You called me once, Lobo
Blanco. Now I call you," intoned Nakaidoklinni. "I
ask you to this last night of a big talk."

"From that hat and shirt you wear, I see you are a
shaman. You have that wolf power I made you long
ago, and it is strong. That is good. I saw you were a
boy who could use it and be something. Your ceremonies and powers are known to me. You can heal and
sing cures and make medicine. Word has come to
my ears of these things. Do not think I haven't
watched you, Young Wolf."

"To this place I have come," said Nakaidoklinni,
"to listen to the land. Four days I have fasted. Many
voices have come to my ears, many words have flowed
through my mind."

"Yes, Shaman. I, too, have seen those things your
eyes saw. I, too, have heard those things your ears
have heard. Your life is one of power and unity. You
have your wickiup and your family, and the earth
provides for your needs. You have raided in Mexico

and became a warrior and followed that way till the trail divided. One way was the shaman way. There you saw a white wolf that you followed. Now your ways are more settled, more at peace, as you gather your herbs, attend to your people's needs. You are a healer of the body, a doctor to the spirit that lives in every heart.

"Now you see the People on a forked path and they don't know which way to go. Both trails lead where no Apache has walked before, so you must choose wisely. The path to the left will lead to good things for the People. The other path will lead to darkness. Both paths have many other branches, both paths have many white men. Choose carefully for all time, choose carefully so the People can live and prosper in this place you call home.

"You, son of Nak-ai-tulan, will be a leader of your people for good or bad. Four things you must do to lead well. Know the white man and his ways. Learn of his power. Keep the People strong in their ways. Remember you, too, are a wolf. The power you have can never be shed." Now the wolf sat silently there, across from Nakaidoklinni. Ever so slowly, the horizon brightened, taking color to give to each thing the new sun saw, taking back all the hues and tints loaned to the black night. When the sun rose, all the things of substance were there in their garments, but across from the shaman he saw only a small ball of white fur. In his ears was the song of the new morning.

I could not help thinking that there was a better way to deal with the Indians than to begin with the conquering sword and follow it up with starvation.

General O. O. Howard,
My Life and Experiences among Our Hostile Indians

The building of the fort and the coming of the soldiers was like learning of fire or the discovery of a new kind of weapon. Once the new thing is known, life is changed and the old way is gone. With the soldiers on the Rio Blanco, the Coyotero way was promised protection from white settlers and miners so life could go on as before. Yet how could it? Before, there were no soldiers to give meat to the people. Before, there was no need to account to anyone for the presence of the members of each band. Before, there was no one who cared to give permission to leave the reservation. Before, there was no reservation. Before, there was no one to stop a group of warriors from raiding where they chose. Before, a good raid could supply a band for a year, give horses to pay for a wife, provide experiences to make a boy a man, earn wealth that was necessary for the family to give the puberty ceremony for their daughters.

Now life would be as before, except that it wasn't. There was a victor and a vanquished. Now the People cut wood and hay to sell to the fort because now there was money. The fort became the center of existence, and things happened there that affected the lives of all. There the words were spoken that formed and sculpted the daily patterns of existence. The reservation boundaries might be established by executive order, or the boundaries might be changed. Perhaps some powerful person or group would come to the fort on a mission of peace or war against one band or another. But what was executive order? What was boundary? Where did these people come from, and what did they represent? The People lived on a rock that was in a giant's hand. How tall was the giant? How many were there like him? To ask these questions was to ask what the eagle sees from on high or what the trees remember. This is how life carried on as before.

The bands of the People were only loosely allied with each other, and each band spoke for only itself. The Coyoteros had made their peace, and the fort was the monument to that reality. Other bands, though, had not spoken the words of peace. These the soldiers chased and hunted in a round of raid and reprisal, killing and burning, starvation and terror. How were the Coyoteros to deal with these other bands, who warred on the soldiers, who raided as before? This is how life carried on unchanged.

Nakaidoklinni saw this and tried to puzzle out the meanings of these things so the Apache would not be as the ant hill that's always being stirred by a boy's stick. He would know the white man, and the knowing would be another power acquired, just like wind power, or the power to see events far away. This knowing would make the People stronger.

One day the fort said that another man was coming to make peace with the other bands and that he wanted all the band chiefs to meet with him. This man was named General Howard, and first he went to Fort Grant to meet with Eskiminzin and the Aravaipa bands, and then he came to Camp Apache to meet with the Coyoteros. Many of the people from Long Ears' camp went to see this general and to hear his words.

The Rio Blanco at Camp Apache was confined to a deep narrow canyon cut through solid rock. The cottonwood trees looked small when viewed from the canyon rim, the stream mostly hidden by dense foliage. Downstream, another fork flowed into the river, and here the canyon opened out into a shallow crossing from where the people made their way up a long slope leading to the buildings and parade ground. The fort was open on all sides and consisted mostly of tents, with a few log-constructed buildings on the south and west sides. Corrals and stock pens were built to the north of the parade ground. High above fluttered the flag that the soldiers always carried with them.

The soldiers were all wearing their blue uniforms, with their best pants and shirts, and the Apaches had dressed in their best, too. Every man carried weapons, though this was an attempt to be fully dressed rather than an act of hostility. In front of the administration building was a long hitching post with a juniper tree at each end, and in front of this a raised platform had been built for the speakers to address the people. A cloudless day looked down on the fort, the grasses were still green, and the yucca stalks were well formed, with buds swelling large and a few white blossoms peeking out here and there.

In front of the platform were some split logs for the people to sit on, and to either side were squads of soldiers. To the left were the horse soldiers and to the right were the foot soldiers, each with flags flying. The logs were nearly full, so Long Ears led his group to the rear, where some squatted on the ground or stood and watched the soldiers and the few white women that were there.

Some officers walked out of the administration building, and immediately a bugle began to blow. The soldiers formed up in rows, various orders being given to each group. As the officers inspected each squad of men, they came to attention and presented arms until all had been inspected and the officers ascended the platform to the front. The bugler blew another call, and all the soldiers stood at attention, their fingers over their eyes. All the Apaches were turning to see what the soldiers were looking at, but all that could be seen were three far-off turkey vultures circling in the sky.

General Crook, the *nantan* with the black beard, stood up in front and said some words that were made into Apache by the scout Cooley. He welcomed the people who had come today, nodding to each band, recognizing each chief. He said many words about peace with the Coyotero and the wishes of the Great White Father for peace with all bands so that all people could live without fear or hunger. Apaches, he said, could make peace with the white government or could have war—it was for them to choose. He said that if it was to be war, the soldiers would not rest until every man was hunted down and killed, every wickiup burned, and all the fields and caches were destroyed so the hostiles who remained would have nothing left but to freeze and starve. Then he warned that any Apache who assisted hostile bands would also be considered hostile. Long Ears' band wondered why the *nantan* was talking like this when they had made their peace and allowed this fort to be built on the Rio Blanco. The words of General Crook did not comfort them.

Next, General Crook said that the Great White Father had sent another general to the Apache to attempt to make peace with all the bands. This man was a peace commissioner, and Crook said many things about General Howard, most of which the bands did not understand. When he finished, all the soldiers hit their hands together, making a great noise, and again Long Ears' people cast around nervously, trying to see what to make of this noise.

General Howard stood there now, and he only had one arm. He said some words, so quietly that each person strained to hear him, but the other officers took off their hats as General Howard fell to his knees, raised his one arm above his head, again looked to the sky, and began to bellow in a great voice. "He makes medicine against us," yelled Sanchez, and all the bands started running for their horses so that no one was left on the logs in front of the general on his knees.

Laughing soldiers stood in the ranks and sat their horses as General Crook ran after the scattered bands. Cooley at his heels yelling, *"Yushde, yushde,"* until they caught up with Diablo, whose band was mounting their horses preparing to leave. Cooley explained that this was the way white men prayed to their gods and that General Howard had done this so the talks would go well and not to make medicine against the People. Cautiously, people peeked out from behind buildings and trees, hesitantly returning to the split logs to hear more words of the general with one arm, and Cooley promised that he would not get on his knees again.

General Howard said that he had been sent by the

white chief to make peace with all the bands of the Apache, not just the Coyotero. The Great White Father knew that a bigger reservation had to be made for all the bands, and this was to be done, with the boundaries being extended to take in Camp Grant and the Aravaipa country. He would be going to Fort Verde, Fort Whipple, and Fort McDowell to talk to other bands, and then would return to his big pueblo, Washington. He said that it was his hope that several Coyotero chiefs would go with him to meet with the Great White Father and other white chiefs there in Washington. Crook, he said, had recommended to him that Diablo, Pedro, Miguel, and Long Ears be taken on this journey. They would be gone maybe two moons, but then they would come back after their talk with the Great White Father.

So this meeting was done. General Howard visited the other forts, returning when the fruits were large. The Coyotero leaders made ready to go with the general, but Long Ears suffered an accident. His horse had fallen on him, crushing his leg. At his request, Nakaidoklinni was asked to go in his place, and to this he readily assented, knowing that he would learn many things about the white man and have many questions answered.

Chief Irotaba had returned from his visit to the "Great Father"
at Washington in safety. He was said to have made on his return
the usual speech to his people comparing the number of pale faces
he met to the leaves of the trees and the sands of the desert. He
informed them that New York was the greatest rancheria in the
world, and that all the soldiers dressed just alike and that their
guns in Washington were just like the guns used by them in
Arizona. He was thus convinced that they were all the same people
and that it was no use to fight them more.

Daniel Ellis Connor,
Joseph Reddeford Walker and the Arizona Adventure

Twenty-five men rode out of Camp Apache to the
dusty creak of wagons and the ring of shod hooves.
Nakaidoklinni, riding in an ambulance drawn by six
mules, watched the scene as from afar. He saw General Howard, the drivers of three wagons, and a small
detachment of escort soldiers with their passengers:
ten Indians, including leaders of the Apaches, Pa-
pagos, Yavapais, and Pimas. He wondered where this
road would lead.

Day followed day, and he sat on the wooden seat
of the wagon, bouncing and jolting until his bones
and joints screamed to walk, and then he would run
off to the side to limber his body. He wished he
had brought his pony, but the only ones riding were
the escorts.

The course followed a northeastly direction over

very broken ground, at first heavily forested, then thinning till a high open tableland was reached where a tree could hardly be seen in any direction. Nakaidoklinni had never been to this country, but he recognized it as the way to Zuni, where many Apaches had gone to trade; many times he had heard these trips described in the wickiups of his people. He often saw game, the deer and elk thinning with the forest until the flat land was gained, where herds of antelope kept a wary and curious distance.

The words of the soldiers were strange to his ears, but he listened for the patterns, looking for tone or inflection, for words repeated that he had heard before. Painfully, with agonizing slowness he began to make a bag of those words that he would keep and silently roll on his tongue, taking one out and trying another as the wagons rolled across the plain. He would practice saying the white man words when he ran, speaking softly to himself so that no one heard or knew.

At camp each evening white man food was prepared. A long piece of canvas was spread on the ground, and for each man there was a plate with the tools that he was to use in eating. The food was strange to Nakaidoklinni's taste, but he took in all that was new, storing each thing away, being like the wolf who always watches, always learns. Each night when the food was ready, General Howard spoke his god words, and the shaman, with the others, learned to stand with an uncovered head as was the white man way.

On the fifth day the canyons began to deepen, the hills rising to the east, forming cliffs. The party camped at Zuni that night, pushing on the next day toward the Rio Puerco; the Rio Grande; Albuquerque, where the soldiers got drunk; and then on to Santa

Fe, beyond which was land unknown to Nakaidoklinni or any of his band.

The road from Santa Fe continued on a northeast course for several more days, traversing wooded, mountainous country until a high pass was crossed and, for the first time in his life, Nakaidoklinni looked to a horizon devoid of mountains, a broad plain expanding before his eyes, as flat as the great waters that some raiders had seen far down in Mexico. In his heart he was adrift in a land with no known landmarks, the still-familiar night sky being his only reminder of home.

Talking was difficult in this odd party traveling across the prairie. The white man spoke his language, the Apaches spoke theirs, and then there were the Pima and Papago and Yavapai tongues. Many spoke some Mexican words, and one of the scouts had been brought along who could translate white man words to Apache. Signs were the common language that all resorted to when other attempts met with frustration.

General Howard had a genuine interest in the chiefs in his charge. He showed Nakaidoklinni how to hold the fork and knife, and often spoke to him, accompanied with much shaking of the head, contortions of the face, waving of the hands, as if Nakaidoklinni could understand. Then he would move on to Pedro or Miguel and have one of his talks with them. The general was a tall, well-built man with full beard and dark hair beginning to turn to gray. He had kind eyes and a quick smile and liked to lead by example, showing the chiefs how each man had to work to get wood for the fire, to push wagons up steep hills, to fold up the canvas or wash the dishes. He told them of losing his arm in the war between the blue and gray soldiers and of the many other tribes of Indians he had seen. But Nakaidoklinni was most interested in the general's Bible. Every seven days the general halted and would not travel. Nakaidoklinni had never seen a book before, so it was with fascination that he watched the general open his Bible, saying words from it as his finger moved down one page and to the next. This Bible had pictures that the general would hold up or pass around, and all the chiefs wondered at these scenes captured on those flat thin sheets. "These are the words of God," General Howard explained. "I have met this God and talk with him daily. He made all that there is and is all-powerful. It was my God that brought me through the great war with only a missing arm. It was God that led me to the Apache, for there I have work to do for Him." Nakaidoklinni heard these words, listening like a wolf as the general spoke of God and power.

At the town of Pueblo, Nakaidoklinni saw the iron tracks of the railroad. He walked the ties, feeling the spikes, seeing the iron road disappear in the distance. Not until a locomotive steamed into view did the meaning of the long iron come to him. An engineer hung out of the locomotive, people were clearly in the cars, and General Howard said that they would leave the wagons and mules here and ride on the train. Nakaidoklinni stared at the noisy monster, steam belching from its boilers, thinking of the dream he had told to Nasta of the man walking on a cloud. Now he would walk on a cloud to see the white chief!

A car was reserved for the party by General Howard. With foreboding, the chiefs were urged aboard, feeling more of their power sucked away into the white world as they choked down their fear, blindly trusting General Howard to deliver them from the bowels of the belching iron horse. The whistle blew, the car lurched, and Nakaidoklinni watched as the Pima chiefs ducked their heads while covering their faces, nearly burrowing under their seats, and there they stayed while the train puffed and whistled its way from Pueblo and out onto the Great Plains pulling east, day and night, pulling east. The wolf in Nakaidoklinni saw that he too had fear in his heart. He sat there stiff as a dried hide, hands hooked onto the seat before him. His eyes were fixed through the window, toward the east. His mind rode on a cloud toward an unknown place with no mountains.

· · · · · · · · · · · · ·

From this time on Nakaidoklinni was in a dream place. Everywhere the train took him there were strange sights for which there were no names: places without names. How could he tell his people where he had been so that they would understand? The words did not exist. The dream was not one that had ever been dreamed in Apacheria. No shaman would recognize its symbols. But everywhere the dream took him there were white men, working in their fields, riding in their wagons, walking in their streets, living in their houses in bigger and bigger pueblos. Though the general gave the names of many things that they saw, the names were as hoots of the owl. What meaning did they have to an Apache? Each day Nakaidoklinni longed for the night when he could again dream Apache dreams.

With the dawn of each day, Nakaidoklinni would cut another notch on a stick he had cut before leaving Camp Apache. On the day he made his twenty-first mark the train pulled into the place the general named New York. Here the train once more spit them out upon the ground. With relief, they stood on shaky legs, attempting to ignore the throngs of people pointing and staring in their direction. The general was their leader. To him they stuck close, never letting him pass from their sight. Here each man was given white man clothes to wear. A whirlwind of visions came to the eye as the general took them on a round of the wonders of the New York pueblo. Most impressive to the medicine man was the wide blue water with the towering ships. Here was the end of the land. With relief he knew that the railroad would take him no farther to the east, no farther from home.

From New York the train took them to the pueblo of the Great White Father, to the place called Washington. Here Nakaidoklinni cut fourteen more notches on his day stick, each day seeing more ships, more buildings, more people.

General Howard named the Great White Father "President Grant," and a day was set for their meeting with him. Each chief made a little talk to the white leader and presented him with a bow or basket or something of their people. These gifts being formally received by President Grant, he would step forward and place a peace medal around the neck of the speaker, saying all men were brothers and could live together in harmony. He asked if their reservations were large enough and some other questions about Camp Apache and seemed very interested in whether the other bands would soon make peace.

"Return to your people and tell them of the ways of the white man, the size of our cities, the wealth of our country. Say that this is the country of your people also and that everyone is of the same government, subject to the same laws. Say that the power of the army cannot be resisted without paying a terrible price in blood and suffering. Say that many peoples make up this nation and that the place of the Indian is reserved with honor and respect." With this the president shook each man's hand and departed the room.

. . . .

For Nakaidoklinni, two other events occurred in Washington that stood out in his mind. The day after seeing the president, the party was treated to the entertainment of a magician who had much power. Many of the chiefs were called upon to assist in the acts, and Nakaidoklinni was chosen to keep track of a pea that was placed under a shell. Every time he picked the shell that held the pea, it was gone. Miguel, who had been fitted for a glass eye in New York, was also brought up to the front. The magician took the glass eye and wrapped it in a scarf and placed it in his hat. Holding it high above Miguel's head, he had the old chief remove the scarf. Shaking it out, a white bird flew out, to Miguel's amazement. Seizing the hat, the perplexed Miguel turned it inside out, demanding the return of his eye. Chasing the magician around the stage, the angry Miguel was even more surprised when, at the magician's urging, the eye was found in the pocket of the chief's coat.

Diablo was called upon to examine a large wooden box into which a lady was placed. A sharp saw was brought on for Diablo's examination, and he said it was sharp. As the lady wiggled her toes and waved her arms, the magician cut her in two. Nakaidoklinni did not know what to do and thought that General Howard would stop the sacrifice, but the general just looked on with interest, not seeming to be concerned. A long white sheet was shaken over the box. Nakaidoklinni could see that the woman's feet and hands moved no more. Lights were dimmed as a candle was brought in to set on the coffin, the magician calling out to his companion, obviously beginning to panic, realizing his deed. Louder, louder he called, running around in circles and holding his head until Nakaidoklinni could take it no more. The magician urged Diablo to open the box, to try to save the woman, but Apaches are afraid of the dead and Diablo was looking for the door, for once not waiting for the general. Just as he got to the door, it opened. There, right in front of him, stood the dead woman's ghost. Quickly he turned to escape, being chased back onto the stage, where he passed through the curtains and out the back. The ghost stopped next to the man who had killed her. Taking out his wand he said words over her to bring her back to the living. Then he threw some scarves on her and everyone could see that she once again lived, as the scarves did not pass through her body but stayed on her flesh and bones. This, thought Nakaidoklinni, is very great medicine indeed!

The day before they were to leave, the general took them to a revival meeting. In front of the tent Nakaidoklinni saw a picture of a man nailed to a cross, blood dripping from his hands and feet. This, he learned, was the son of the white god who was killed on the cross, but then also returned to the living. Later, the preacher in the tent talked of this man, saying that every man could be reborn again to the living if only he believed in this god. He said the power of the god was in his hands, and these he used to cure people as they came up asking his help. General Howard told the chiefs that the power of the white medicine man was big because his god was big and was the one true god. Nakaidoklinni heard these words like a wolf, keeping them aside where those things were put that helped explain the power of the white man.

The time in Washington was over. The train was boarded to make the long trip west. Through the long days, the mechanical monotony of the wheels on the tracks added to the dreamlike quality of what the chiefs had seen. Their world had opened for them, each now knowing more of the extent of its boundaries, each feeling diminished as an Apache. What once had seemed the vast land of the People was a small corner of the world settled by folk who never had heard of White Painted Woman or Slayer of Monsters.

Riding west on a cloud! Nakaidoklinni told General Howard that he would know more of the great white god. The general commended him and they agreed that this would be seen to in Santa Fe.

If he had not gone to Washington and seen President Grant; if he had not picked up a smattering of Christianity in Santa Fe . . . if, in short, he had remained the kindly White Mountain herb doctor he was in 1871, Cibique Creek would not have become a battleground.

Thomas Cruse,
Apache Days and After

Santa Fe. How insignificant it seemed in comparison to the cities of the east. For two moons the shaman was placed in the care of Father Vargas at the church of San Miguel. Nakaidoklinni had only a meager grasp of English, but enough that a crude understanding could sometimes be communicated, especially when embellished by gesture and signs. His Mexican words, the tongue of his father, were useful too, but he knew few of these. He had learned a smattering from captive women and children adopted as Apaches. Still, each day brought more illumination of the white man's god and the powers of his religion.

The Jesus hung on an ornately carved cross, staring down with empty eyes from high above the altar. "Why," thought Nakaidoklinni, "do the white men keep this reminder of death about them?" No Apache would stay around the body of a dead person. If someone died in a wickiup, it would be burned to free the spirit and all of that person's possessions burned as well, even the name dying in the flames. The hoot of an owl, the ghostly sound of the departed, was reason to move a wickiup, change a camp. Yet here was the home of the dead Jesus, his body and name glorified and remembered. Nakaidoklinni was unsettled by this and averted his eyes when in the church, but the wolf in him studied that Christ, recording the movements of the priests, the sounds of the bells, the prayers of the people.

Santa Fe gave Nakaidoklinni the opportunity to digest the meanings, the revelations of the trip to the east. The power of the blue soldiers was a power of vast numbers. When in battle with a company of cavalry the numbers could be equal or even favorable to the Apaches. A raid could cast Apache numbers in greatly advantageous terms. But how could the Apaches hope to prevail against a people as numerous as he now knew the whites were? Accommodation was not a behavior that the People were used to when confronted with might and aggression, but now there was clearly no other choice. Yes, the white man's power was one of vastly superior numbers.

In the east, General Howard had taken the chiefs to naval yards, military garrisons, factories where munitions and armaments were made, and this, too, was a power of the whites that could not be opposed. The People lived with the land and were governed by it. The white world was one where nature was the servant rather than the master. Water flowed from pipes, wires carried messages, people moved on clouds, whether across the prairie or on the blue waters. These people built houses and buildings and cities and lived on the land, not in the land. "This is white man way, not Apache way," thought Nakaidoklinni, "but still a source of power far beyond the reckoning of the people of the Rio Blanco." He knew that these ways of the white man would be even more difficult for his people to comprehend than their numbers.

And now he was learning about another source of the white man power. This was not a power of powder and steel, or the triumph of the white world over the powers of the earth. No, this was the power of the whites over the heavens. Whether they owned their god or that god owned them he could not tell, but the priests and preachers never mentioned White Painted Woman and were always quick to say that their god was the one true god that must be acknowledged by all.

"All other gods are false and must be cast down," explained Father Vargas. "Believe in Jesus, who died and rose again from the dead, and you will live forever." The father talked of the power of the Lord, the compassion of Mary, and the wrath of God, so terrible that everything before it was as dust before the wind.

In every wickiup each generation was told the stories of long, long ago so that every Apache knew how the People had been created, how the world had come about. Beyond this the relationship to nature and the cosmos was a personal one having to do with the acquisition of power, such as wolf power, wind power, horse power, witch power. From what Nakai-doklinni could tell, the white man did not know of these things. His questions about the powers of witches disturbed the father, leading him to cross himself, to murmur prayers that were not known, to Nakaidoklinni. The white man, though, seemed to share the same god to which they talked individually and personally or sometimes through the fathers. Nakai-doklinni tried to understand who this god was, but it was confusing. Sometimes Vargas talked of "our father in heaven" and later he would speak of "Jesus, the son of God," and many of the white man prayers were to Mary, the mother of Jesus.

Father Vargas spent hours in the quiet afternoons telling Nakaidoklinni of the miracles of the Bible, but these were not mysterious or surprising to the medicine man. These things were known to the People and at first he would tell the father of his own miracles, but these were discouraged by the priest and Nakaidoklinni could tell that the father did not understand his stories.

Many were the times that the shaman asked questions of the father, trying to clarify some aspect of the white man belief and leading the father to long, elaborate explanations, going far beyond the question, far beyond the understanding of Nakaidoklinni. Usually the father came back to the promise of redemption, the reality of resurrection, the hope of eternal life. Sometimes he spoke of stories of long, long ago and how belief in the white man god delivered whole peoples from oppression and bondage. These stories Nakaidoklinni listened to, carefully putting them away so he would have them for his own.

As the days got shorter, a chill infused the night air. Over ninety marks were notched in Nakaidoklinni's time stick when Father Vargas told him that it was time for him to return to his people. On the following day a corporal came for him, and in fourteen more days he was back to Camp Apache. The sky held a deep blue, the season being When the Earth Is Reddish Brown.

"Why, Smith, where did you get those heads?"

"These is the heads we killed this morning," he replied without taking his eyes off of them. "Well, what in the devil did you bring them here for?" was again asked. "To git the brains to tan my deer hides with, what you 'pose?" he answered quietly. "The best buckskin I ever seed," he continued, "was tanned with Ingun brains." Ingun . . . he gave a little chortle and consoled himself by saying that before that rancheria could bother any more, a new "crop of Inguns" would have to be planted there.

Daniel Ellis Connor,
Joseph Reddeford Walker and the Arizona Adventure

Nakaidoklinni returned to a country at war. The mission of General Howard had been generally a failure. He had been successful in meeting with band chiefs who were already at peace, but made few inroads among the hostiles. Upon Howard's return to the east, General Crook seized the opportunity of having units in the field at all times. By now, a string of forts and camps encircled the Tonto Basin and the Pinal Mountains, along with the drainages of the Rio Salado, Rio Verde, and Gila. Inside was a tortured land extending from desert arroyo to deep, forested canyons, unmapped and unknown except to the Apaches. Though each band was safe in the fastness of its territory, any raid to the outside that left tracks invited retribution from the soldiers. Through a series of raids and counterattacks that had occurred throughout the summer, many rancherias had been located and destroyed. The dead warriors were left to rot where they had fallen; any women and children captives were herded to Fort McDowell or to Camp Grant.

General Crook took to the field with his men. He would talk to hostile bands at every opportunity, stressing that his objective was peace. Frequently he would release old women or young boys, telling them to say to their people that they would be allowed to surrender and receive rations as long as they ceased raiding and killing but that if they kept to their ways the soldiers would trail them, burning their fields and wickiups and supplies until only starvation was left. And General Crook was one to keep his word, so his threats were always backed up with teeth.

Early on in his command he discovered that to fight Apaches the soldiers must be kept in the field constantly, traveling light and fast, and that two things could guarantee success; the first was a well-equipped string of pack mules to supply the men in the field, and the second was the assistance of Apache scouts to track and locate the hostile bands. For the latter, he depended heavily on the peaceful Coyoteros, who found themselves to be the corn ground by the mano of the soldiers on the metate of the renegade bands. Time and again the peaceful bands were told that if they were not with the army, they were against them. Thus it was that in the late fall of that year, November 1872 by the white man count, Nakaidoklinni and Sanchez found themselves joining Company A, White Mountain Scouts, for a six-month enlistment under Captain George Randall of the Twenty-third Infantry, Camp Apache, Arizona Territory.

Camp Apache was situated in a beautiful spot. It

sat between the forks of the Rio Blanco on the margin where the high yucca desert turned to juniper and piñon trees. On the slope to the north of the camp tall pines were to been seen, this being a region of deep winter snows and cool summers. To the west was the Tonto Basin, a dry land broken by occasional rivers and springs, a country of mazes, of canyon, plateau, mesa, and butte.

Before leaving, Captain Randall talked to the scouts. "You men will be the eyes and ears of the soldiers. We will cross the southern end of the Tonto Basin on a route to Fort McDowell. To avoid detection, the soldiers will move only at night. Watch for any tracks, any fires, any sign that will lead us to hostile rancherias and report back to me."

The soldiers and scouts traveled together the first day. On the second day, the Apache scouts split up, riding out, searching for the enemy. Sanchez and Nakaidoklinni rode out together, checking back each evening, leading the soldiers on that night. In the drainage of Cherry Creek sign became more common, but nothing was recent. Still, each southerly step toward the Rio Salado led the soldiers deeper into the fastness that the Apaches had always held as their own.

Now the scouts started reporting abandoned wicki-ups in small rancherias, and the soldiers redoubled their efforts to remain hidden. On Captain Randall's orders, no shots were to be fired for any reason short of attack. Each camp was made in sheltered canyons hidden from the higher surrounding mountains. Fires were kept small, built of dry wood, always protected from the vigilant eyes of renegade bands.

Nine days out, one of the scouts reported sighting a campfire west of Tonto Creek. Randall passed word to the soldiers to be ready to move out at dark. He told the men to remain as silent as possible and to not strike any matches. It was a long cold night, as the men had to go without the comfort of the pipe.

Nakaidoklinni and the other scouts were leading the way. About two hours before dawn they approached the desert arroyo where the fire had been sighted. Other flames were seen to flicker in the chill air, and a light smoky haze hugged the ground. Word was passed to dismount.

Three men were left with the horses, while the soldiers and scouts proceeded on foot. The night was black and the going was slow as the attackers moved up a slope favored by towering saguaros and patches of cholla, and then down into a bottom of mesquite and palo verde. Now the men could wind the smoke from the camp.

The scouts moved into position on the hill to the west of the wickiups, taking up position among some boulders halfway down the slope. The night was still dark, though dawn was not far off. Across, on the far hill, the soldiers were to move into position and then wait until light. The night was utterly still and quiet. No movement could be seen below. Nakaidoklinni crouched behind a boulder, sighting between it and a saguaro on his right, taking in the blackness, ignoring the cold from the rocks and the earth. A pale glow could be seen to the east. Some faint stars winked out till the next evening. Forty rifles stared down on the glowing embers, anxious, waiting to see what would be revealed. Gradually, the night lifted her folds so that here and there a shape took form where before had only been black. A wickiup. Some baskets. Some strips of meat hanging from a mesquite. Two more wickiups. Some ponies up the canyon. Some more wickiups tucked in the desert brush watched now by only a few stars overhead. Still the rifles silently peered down.

An ancient one slowly emerged from a wickiup stretching old bones, limbering up for the new day, throwing a small bundle of kindling on the embers. Still the guns looked down, the front sights clear now. Shooting light! Killing light nearly at hand, each man ready to strike, coiled like a rattler, till finally the captain's clear steady voice cried, "Fire!" and a leaden rain pounded the wickiups. Yelling voices, barking dogs, people running for their lives, trying to find the way out of the cross fire, some with weapons but most just running, already conceding this day to the soldiers, already thinking of revenge.

Nakaidoklinni was in a trance, seeing this warrior, this woman, this child through the narrow field of iron sights. A well-placed Apache camp should be near a rocky hill that would afford cover and escape. This camp was well placed. Each person bursting from a wickiup first made for the rocks, to be cut down in the withering fire from above. Those who could, ran up the canyon and into the brush, and from there some escaped. But through his sights Nakaidoklinni saw men and women fall. This one struggled with a broken leg. That one sang a death song. Some never moved again. Then the storm lifted, the day brightened, the rain and hail grew intermittent, the thunder receded in the distance. The bloody flash flood had passed, and the soldiers were walking among the wickiups rounding up survivors. Fifteen of the band were killed, laid out in a row. Twelve were captured, huddled together in a circle on the sand. One by one the wickiups were torched, extra camp supplies thrown onto the inferno. The lives of the camp were reduced to ashes to be blown across the hills, to be washed to the Tonto, to return to the precious waters of this arid land.

The position of the soldiers had been given away by the sounds of battle, the smoke of the wickiups. Captain Randall kept the men on the trail to Fort McDowell for most of that day. Another freshly abandoned rancheria was passed, apparently warned by the morning's battle. It too got the torch. There was to be no quarter in the campaigns of that winter. Other means had been tried and had failed, said Randall. It was General Crook's intention to bring the hostiles to their knees through starvation, freezing, and terror.

The scouts rode out ahead, finding fresh sign of the departing camp, but the band had split up, each going his own way to rendezvous at some previously agreed-upon place. From the peaks and mesas, smoke told of the soldiers' presence. The scouts knew that the remainder of the trip to McDowell would be uneventful, and so it was.

. . . .

Fort McDowell was built in a forest of saguaro and mesquite on a plain overlooking the Rio Verde. Randall's command stayed at the fort for the next two weeks, laying over to resupply and to give the men and their mounts a rest. For the soldiers it was the season of Christmas.

While at McDowell a dispatch was received that two companies of the Fifth Calvary from Camp Grant had combined with an expedition from Fort McDowell and had attacked the camp of Nanni Chaddi, hidden deep in the canyons of the Rio Salado. An early-morning siege of their cavelike fortress had succeeded in wiping out the whole band. Seventy-six were killed, with twenty women and children captives. Great stores of supplies were destroyed. Randall's command was still at Fort McDowell when Captain Burn's command rode in with the captives. Most were wounded, the survivors being a sullen and defeated group.

From McDowell, Randall led his men on a triangular path back to the upper reaches of the Rio Verde and over to the Rio Salado staying out two or three weeks at a time, then returning to Fort McDowell for more supplies. This was a harsh time of year, and twice they were caught in winter snows. One storm moved fast, but the other settled in, snowing for the better part of two days. When the sky finally cleared, the snow was up to the knees. Scout and soldier were chilled and wet, wishing for the fires of home, but on they trod, finding here or there an abandoned wickiup or maybe some ponies.

On the way back to McDowell, three hungry women walked in asking for food. They were fed and taken back to the fort. Whenever other commands were met, word was traded of camps attacked, each resulting in a few more dead hostiles, with the numbers slowly adding up to heavy losses for the Tonto bands.

In early March, once again back at Fort McDowell, the telegraph from Fort Whipple told of an Apache attack at Walnut Grove. A young miner had been captured, stripped, and tortured till he died. When a search party found him, his body was shot with more than fifty arrows, each deliberately placed so as not to kill. The man had writhed on the ground, breaking the shafts, turning the points until he had bled to death. The Apaches had then attacked a stage, killed three more, and disappeared east toward the Tonto.

Randall hurriedly moved his men out, but several

had been on a binge and were not fit to walk or ride. The scouts were told to bring up the rear to make sure there were no laggards. For miles, some of the soldiers kept dropping off their mounts, saying that they just needed to rest. Two were tied to mules, hauled into the first night's camp, and dumped with the rest of the baggage.

Randall led the men through the Mazatzal Mountains north to Tonto Creek, encountering no hostiles. Near the point where the camp had been attacked and burned in December, they turned west, skirting a broad valley that climbed up into the junipers. Here fires had been built recently. Some tracks no more than four or five days old had been made by a small party of five or six Indians. This path led higher to the west and over to the drainage of the Verde.

Randall had his men moving at night now, the scouts out in the day searching for dust, smoke, or other signs to lead them on. He thought the small group was returning to their band and that it would be best to follow slowly, avoiding detection, and that then they would be led to the band and be able to attack a larger group. The soldiers kept to the deep canyons, letting the scouts show the way. Now the track led south to a vast no-man's-land of hills and canyons, covered with saguaro and mescal on the lower reaches, mesquite and juniper on the higher slopes. Many small streams sang their way to the Rio Verde, as this was the time of year when the snows were still melting, new storms occasionally blowing in with fresh rain. South the track led, following the course of the river but keeping to a high bench on the east side. The Rio Verde had cut a sharp, deep canyon, the river's lush margins clothed in cottonwood or willow, the upslope turning to mesquite, prickly pear, and the tall branching saguaro. Cliffs above the river were formed of red granite or, alternately, by white chalk. Everywhere was rock, soil being scarce.

One evening, two Carrizo scouts brought in a woman and her baby whom they had captured on a trail leading from the river. Captain Randall questioned her about the location of her band but was met with an impassive silence. Randall directed a group of the soldiers to secure the woman, while he removed the cradleboard. Then he had the translator say to her that she must lead the soldiers to the rancheria or her baby would be given to one of the Coyotero scouts. Bitterly the woman agreed to lead them to her camp. The woman said it was a half day's march to the rancheria, and Randall directed his men to move out. She went ahead with the company of scouts, leading across the river to the west, where the sun had already set.

A series of canyons riddled the country, leading from a high tableland of juniper and oak to the desert floor of the Rio Verde. The soldiers found themselves climbing a broad, rocky valley heading to the northeast. The going was painfully slow, picking out the faint trail while avoiding the cactus and bushes, nearly all of which had thorns. Of the destination, nothing could be glimmered. Ahead was just more rising valley silhouetted against a faint sky. A late moon rose to the soldiers' backs, its shadows as a beacon providing edges and substance to the path that must be followed. The command was in a tight string, the scouts to the fore, the soldiers on their mounts, then the pack mules, and the spare mounts brought up the rear. The trail followed a desert stream that splashed and gurgled over rocks only to silently sink into the sands and then reappear at the next outcrop of rock.

The cold moon sailed overhead when the troop topped out of the canyon rim onto a rolling plain. For the first time that night, the eye could look out instead of up. A long broken horizon filled the gaze, with a dark tower in the northwest sky the most prominent feature; a brooding, looming ship in the night, sailing on shadowy waters. Here, the woman said, on its fortress heights was the sanctuary of her band.

Randall directed his soldiers to leave the horses at this point, each man being given pieces of gunny sack with which to wrap his feet. It would take another hour to reach the base of the mesa. Silent stealth would be the hallmark of this march, and talking, smoking, or stumbling was liable to alert the hostile camp. Again the men moved out, single file and ghostlike, keeping to the brushy bottoms, avoiding the ridges, where their silhouettes might be readily detected. Fuzzy stars filled the sky. The moon was ahead of them. Each exhaled breath was a frosty cloud. On they marched, the scrub oak in places being nearly impenetrable. The men were forced to crawl through thorny gorse with twigs and branches plucking for their eyes and ears, thorny leaves and cactus pushing into hands and knees. Silently, each man picked himself up again, moving on so as not to lose the shadowy figure ahead.

The butte they headed for was an abrupt granite outcrop capped with an ancient lava flow. Its sides were nearly vertical, with a steeply curving slope of loose rock anchored only by the brush. The woman was tied and gagged, the scouts leading a winding path up the northeast slope, one halting step at a time. To the north was a narrow canyon, its rushing water masking the sounds of the night. Yet at every loose rock, every broken twig, the men were halted, ducking down in the brush until it seemed all was clear. By the time the north slope was reached, the scouts doubled back in a hairpin approach. The butte was more than halfway mounted as they headed to the crest, where a gate was formed by massive pillars of broken lava. Through a patch of Spanish bayonet and small cholla, one man at a time could just squeeze through to the top, though no sign could be seen of a camp.

The butte was a natural fortress, a stone island rising from the landscape. It offered a vantage over the country for miles in every direction. The summit was narrow, of solid rock, running nearly north to south. To the southern end was a humping outcrop of granite, dividing the top into two parts. All of the command could smell smoke but waited as Sanchez crept through the boulders for a better view to the south. Returning, he reported a small flat end to the butte, and it was there the band was camped.

Whispers passed for the men to fan out, taking to the boulders, and then Randall would give the word, as at the attack on the Tonto band. Silently, the men spread out from east to west, a creeping picket fence of steel blocking the top, springing the trap. Still, nothing could be seen of the Apaches, as each of the attackers began climbing into the boulders, getting into position. Now they waited for the dawning morning. Imperceptibly, one ray at a time, each shade of black faded, paled, and brightened into the new day, the final day for this band of the People.

Nakaidoklinni saw it all and heard each shot. The yell into the camp that they were surrounded and should surrender. The howling anguish of the freshly wakened camp. A shot fired from who knows where. Answering barks, powdered snarls charging from the boulders. Men falling, claimed by a hell storm of bullets. Fleeing people with nowhere to go huddling on the ground, jumping to oblivion, the camp over-whelmed in surprise, never fearing that danger might stalk this fortress sentinel, that all could be lost in the length of a sunrise. But this happened. The band of thirty warriors, well over a hundred people in all, winked out that morning, just like the stars, some never to shine again, never belonging to the same constellations, never to be seen in the same sky.

When all was done, Nakaidoklinni walked among the crude shelters, not really wickiups. Here had been Apaches who had moved to the mountaintops like the Moquis, like the Old Ones who left their stone houses dotting the mesas and the high places. The butte had a grand command of the surrounding Apache country, but could it be Apache country if the People were forced to live in a place like this, on a windswept pile of rock?

The captives were herded together. The pitiful shel-ters, the bodies of the dead, the few stores of mescal and hides were left to the coyotes. White man clothes were found in the camp. The vanquished band said that they had been taken a moon ago in a raid on some white miners south of the town of Prescott.

Randall took his command back to Fort McDowell. His raid on the forlorn butte was to be the last major attack of that campaign. Though they had terrorized and cowed the settlers of central Arizona Territory, the Tonto Apaches had never been numerous, and now their ability as well as their will to fight was de-stroyed. Over the weeks and months that followed, scattered camps and small groups of two, three, or ten would appear at one of the forts ringing the Tonto, declaring defeat, begging clemency, their emaciated bodies speaking eloquently of the condition of their hopes and dreams. The company of Apache scouts and the Twenty-third Infantry returned to Camp Apache, the six-month enlistment coming to an end.

My friend, I have come to surrender my people, because you have too many copper cartridges. I want to be your friend. I want my women and children to be able to sleep at night, and to make fires to cook their food without bringing troopers down on us.

Cha-ut-lipan to General Crook,
from John G. Bourke,
With General Crook in the Indian Wars

"What will you do now, my brother?" asked Sanchez. They had returned to the Rio Blanco, received their pay, and were riding back to the *gota*.

"I have my place. I am a shaman, not a scout. The people ask me to use my power when they are sick, when they are cursed or witched. I have seen that this is what I must do. So it will be."

"Yes, you have your place," agreed Sanchez, and they rode in silence, both men glorying in the sunshine, in the familiarity of the hills where they were born. The Tonto was not their land. It was not known to them and did not speak to them. But here, every mountain had a name, every odd formation of rocks. The clans of the Coyoteros were named for these places because that is where they came from, where they lived, where they belonged. There were the White Water people, the Across the Water people, the Rock Jutting into Water people, the Alders Jutting Out people, and the Slender Peak Standing Up people. There were the Walnut Tree people, the Rock

Encircling people, the Owl's Song people, and the Wild Gourd Growing people. Each clan had its place of origin, and those places were known to all. Right now the men were at the place Two Rows of Yellow Pine Joining, and this place did speak to them. They knew where they were, and that place knew of their passing.

"I am not a shaman," thought Sanchez, half to himself, half aloud. "What place is there for me? I am a warrior. This is what I am for. My fathers and their fathers before them were warriors and raiders. This was in their heart, in their muscle and bone. It was not for them to ask, 'What am I?' They knew what they were. But I must ask, 'What am I?' "

Nakaidoklinni knew that this was a question that each of the People must ask and that the answer would not be easy coming. This question would rip a great hole in the spirit of the people. How could a warrior know of the forces shaping that answer?

"You say you are not a scout, that you are a medicine man. Am I a scout, then? I tracked and trailed those people in the Tonto. My gun spoke with the soldiers. I saw warriors go down from my shots.

"Those people were not Coyoteros. They were not of the Cibique. They were not of the Two Rows of Yellow Pine Joining people. We are several people. There is not one chief. Each band has its leader, each group had its wise man who showed the way. Were we scouts wrong to follow those people for the soldiers? In the past one band has fought another, is this not so? Yet now, this is all there is left to fight. What would the fathers say of this, that we do not go south anymore to kill the *nancin* and win his horses, but that now we go west to attack the Tontos and win the white man money?"

Now they had come to the point overlooking Gambol's Oak Standing. Nakaidoklinni stopped to gaze south, his eyes resting on each hill as he took in the drainage of the Rio Negro. General Howard had said that this land would belong to the People for as long as the water flowed in the streams, as long as the sun rose each day. How would the People pay for this granting of the land that was already theirs, where each different place had been named by Apache tongues long, long ago, back before time.

"Am I to be a farmer, then, Sanchez? My fathers have been fearless chiefs and brave men. We have always eaten of the land. We cut the mescal, dried the fruit of the yucca and the other cactuses, gathered the acorns and pine nuts, and hunted the deer, and when we needed more meat we won it in Mexico. To this was added our corn and the things we grew on the land. But we have not been known as farmers. It is not from us that other people have traded for the corn and squash. It is not the Apache people who have been the bakers of bread and tortillas."

Nakaidoklinni heard the words of Sanchez, but his thoughts were far away because he knew that his friend was thinking out loud, talking to himself. "I, too, must see what my life makes," he thought. "Sanchez says I am a medicine man and feels that the world looks the same as it always has to me, but has he felt the rocks move as I have? Has he seen those things I saw when I went with General Howard? A medicine man is nothing if he cannot cure the patient, if he can't find the source of sickness. But what ails the people now? The sickness that will come will not be the sickness of old. Will the singing of the shaman, the powers of the rattle, the powers of *hodden-tin* be enough to heal the rip in the spirit of the

People? Sanchez says that those people of the Tonto were not our people, and perhaps this so. But they lived in wickiups like we make; they tanned the hide of the deer in the same way; their arrows looked the same. And when the bullets entered their skin they bled the same until the breath left their bodies."

"When I go to the water and see my face in the pool," continued Sanchez, "I see all my fathers behind me, and my heart gets hard. When I hear the spirits of the *Gan* or see the dancers, I think, 'Those were our old gods.' What happened to them? Where did they go? I think, 'Maybe they have deserted the People.'

"I am not like you, my brother. You have powers of the shaman. You go to the top of mountains and speak to the spirits of the people. Who speaks to me and tells me what to do? Who speaks to Sanchez? I am like an elk in a blizzard. My head is down, my eyes are nearly shut, but I keep going, not knowing where. How can I lead my people as my father has?

"The coming of the white man, the coming of the blue soldiers, what does this mean to us? If the old ways are gone, what ways are left? I am not a white man. I do not ride in wagons or follow the plow. I do not dig in the earth for the metal to make a knife. My heart is hard, my brother. My eyes look straight ahead but do not see. It is for you to see where we go, what path is meant for us. The people need their shaman now. Say to us what you see so the path will be clear. Say the words to soften our hearts before they turn to stone."

These words the shaman heard. Nakaidoklinni felt these words of Sanchez. They tore at him like brambles. "That wolf told me that these things would happen," he thought. "Many difficulties I have seen that will afflict my people. Now Sanchez asks me to show the way, but I barely know the direction, still less the names of the rocks and trees along the way. I am a shaman, not Slayer of Monsters. There are no powers I have of my own. The powers I have are the powers that seek me out, that are given to me. Are the old gods gone? I don't know, but I think they are still here. I wonder if they have lost their powers, but how can I say this to Sanchez or any other person? How can I say this to myself?"

Sanchez was still speaking, quietly talking, gesturing with his hands. "What of our children? What of my sons and daughters? The raid is gone. That is how a boy became a man. That is where a man got his wealth. That is why we made our bodies endure, why we ran all day, why we swam in the icy waters of the river. Do we do this so we can go to the fort to get beef? So we can learn to cook flour and bacon? So our men can be scouts for the soldiers? My heart is hard, my brother. Say the words to make it soft, so I can again feel it beat in my chest."

He looked at the shaman riding beside him. Had he heard? Perhaps. But Nakaidoklinni knew that there were many things that each man would have to answer in his own way. The White Wolf Shaman could only cock his head and listen to the voices echoing in the shadows of the homes of the clans. Sometimes he heard nothing. Sometimes he heard faint voices from afar that seemed to be mixed as leaves in a whirlwind. He listened for the strong clear voice that he would know was meant for him.

18

But let us return to the time when the Apaches were still in their wild state, following almost untrammeled and unchecked their murderous career. Arizona is a country where every highway, every path, every hamlet and nearly every rancho could tell, had they the gift of speech, of devilish deeds, of crafty ambuscade, murdered settlers and travelers, unfortunate captives tortured to death in the most cruel manner and then mutilated in a disgusting fashion.

A. M. Gustafson, ed.,
John Spring's Arizona

Time passed. No longer quite Apache time. More so, white man time, folding the Apache into its rhythm. Chains forged of ration days.

Some band would step over the invisible reservation line, go back to old haunts. Maybe some rancher would be killed. More scouts would enlist, six months white man time.

. . . .

The measure of the days was not the seasons, no longer the moons or the time of this or that raid. The days spilled out in tenures of agents, rotations of officers, transfers of companies, the building of road or telegraph. Always the People were subject to words on paper from somewhere afar. Words that could not be read. Words that could not be understood. Words that must be heeded.

"They say that the soldiers will no longer have charge of the Indians, that we will have a civilian agent." These words were on the breeze, infused in the morning mists, rising in the warmth of the day to the farthest canyon until every ear had heard. Soon Agent Roberts came, and now he had the rations at the agency buildings that he put across the Rio Blanco from Camp Apache. So the people went there to get their beef, their flour, their blankets, their metal pots.

"They say that a new agent has been made for the Apache, a man named Clum." And this was so. Clum came to the Rio Blanco and met with the chiefs. He was a cocky, young white man in fringed buckskin who wore a gun on his hip and a pair of white riding gloves.

"When will you move to the agency?" asked Long Ears.

"I plan to stay at San Carlos," Clum replied. "Once a week I will come to bring supplies."

"How does he think he will get here when the snows come?" asked Sanchez. But this was a white man problem. This was for Clum to solve. Let him find the error in his plan. He will discover he has made a mistake.

"Have you heard, my brothers? The soldiers have a paper from the Great White Father who has changed the boundary, made our land smaller."

"Has this land not been given to us?" Ilnaba inquired of her husband. "A peace has settled on the land now that this place has been promised to us. That agreement is made and done. How can the president change what has been settled?"

"They say that the Yavapais are being moved from their camps on the Rio Verde to be kept at San Carlos. Yes, they say this is true."

"The Yavapais!" muttered Diablo. "How can they live there at San Carlos, where they have never lived before? That is not the land of the Yavapais. They are not Apache people. Their tongue is not the Apache tongue."

Then one ration day, there was Clum marking off names of all who were there, seeing how many rations each group would be entitled to. The wagons were uncovered as the chiefs lined up and the members of each band squatted in front of the agency. Clum stood up on one of the wagons, and everyone could see that he was there to make a speech. He started talking to "my Apache brothers and sisters," and there was a stern look on his face.

"My Apache brothers and sisters, I have come to you today to bring these rations and supplies and to give you these beeves, and this makes my heart glad. But I also come because of this paper from the commissioner of Indian affairs in Washington, and it makes my heart ache." Then Clum read that paper to the chiefs. He just read the words as if to white men who knew what he was saying. Then the words were said again so the people would know what the paper said. They said that all the Apache people who lived on the reservation would have to move to San Carlos, and that only in that place would rations be given out and only to the bands who had moved. "This is to begin next ration day," Clum stated to the hushed crowd. He just stood there. No one said anything. There were no words to say. San Carlos! The Coyoteros, the Cibiques, are mountain people. San Carlos is a hot desert land. It has no trees, no deer, no pine nuts, no juniper berries. The names in that places are not the names that the people know, not the home of this people's clans.

At last, Pedro got up and said these things to Clum, that his people knew the San Carlos but that they were not of that place, that their spirits would not be restful there in the desert. He spoke all the things that each person knew deep inside, and Clum stood there, hearing his words until Pedro had finished.

"I, too, know these things that my brother Chief Pedro has said," spoke Clum. "This paper, though, is the word of the Indian commissioner. Who am I to change his orders? These lands of the Rio Blanco will still be set aside for the Apache. This has not changed. This cannot be changed, for the Great White Father has provided these lands for your needs. The commissioner, though, is your friend. His interests are your interests. He wants you to learn to be sufficient unto yourselves. He wants you to always get the supplies and rations that you have coming. This will be easier to provide at San Carlos. There will always be supplies there, and you will be given land to farm so your people will never be hungry."

Then Clum started to give out those supplies that he had brought in the wagons. Each group, as they got their rations, packed them and left until finally there were no more. Clum and the packers from San Carlos prepared to return the way they had come, but before they did, they stacked some hay up next to the agency building, struck a match, and burned that building to the ground.

· · · · · · · · · · · ·

The people of the mountains started trickling to the south, below the Rio Negro, across the Rio Salado, under the Natanes Rim to the broken desert plain where they would never be hungry. Every step of the way the grasses perceptibly turned from a lush green to dry brown until at last the grass was only found in the washes, under the protective branches of the mesquite, the palo verde. The pines and cedars thinned, becoming scrubby, until there were no more, relief to the land being provided now by the saguaro, the ocotillo, the low-growing prickly pear. San Carlos was a thorny place where the juices of life were easily sucked out and dried. In the desert, deep roots were required to survive, but those mountain people blew into that place like tumbleweeds.

Long Ears brought his little band up to the crossing of the Rio Negro; they were a small group of people and horses carrying large baskets stuffed with the few things they owned. The trail was familiar, for this was the way to Mexico. All the raiders had stories of this trail, some their own, some told by the fathers. On they went, climbing out of the canyon, over the plateau, and then down the long drainage toward the San Carlos and the Gila, winding on through the yucca and mesquite. It was hot. The corn in the fields they had abandoned were forming tassels; the season of growth. But the desert had a shimmering dryness. The fruits of the saguaro were already turning red and withering. The snakes and other animals of the land started coming out at dark, keeping to the shade or the den in the heat of the day. Yet down that long divide Long Ears brought his people, to the sands of the Rio San Carlos, then upstream, passing wickiups, passing the white rows of tents of the soldiers, approaching the parade ground beyond which was the flagpole and the adobe agency buildings.

Nakaidoklinni followed Long Ears, watching his chief's heavy steps, feeling the agony of forcing one foot to lead the other away from the well-watered Cibique to this place. A halting breeze blew across the trail, providing some relief from the choking dust. "There is no life to this place," thought Nakaidoklinni. The people were apparently inside their wickiups avoiding the heat. Here and there was a burro, a dog seeking shade, trying to find energy to bark, giving up the effort. Looking ahead, Nakaidoklinni could see the agency building clearly now. It was a long, squat adobe with doors at each end of the front, opening out onto a covered porch set with benches. An *olla* hung from the beams with a gourd dipper hanging to its side. An open window was behind it, but Nakaidoklinni could not see anything through the window.

Suddenly, Nakaidoklinni was aware that Long Ears had stopped and was looking toward the flagpole. Nakaidoklinni gave him a questioning look and the chief flicked his head, his lips pointing to something on the ground, something that almost looked like shriveled pumpkins, something that might have been pieces of meat left over from ration day if it hadn't been for the hair, for the head bands. But there was no mistaking that the pumpkins were the heads of seven Apaches who had been carefully lined up in obedience to the flag, though two or three were knocked over, ears chewed off by the camp dogs and coyotes. Nakaidoklinni could see a long line of ants that passed in review by the heads and wound off into the brush. These and a cloud of flies seemed to be the sum of life in that place.

Long Ears turned, moving on toward the adobe, tying his horse to the rail in front, entering the door on the left because it was the one with a sign overhead. Nakaidoklinni entered too, but no one was to be seen, so they returned to the porch, taking up positions on the benches, all of the band sitting or squatting in the shade, each eye set to look away from that flagpole. Before long they could see Clum crossing the parade ground with two other men, one an interpreter they knew and the other an officer who was new to them.

Clum welcomed the band, writing down the name of each person. Long Ears was told that he could make a camp on the San Carlos upstream about three miles and that a wagon would follow with rations for his band. It was Clum who brought up the heads. He said that they were the heads of the outlaw Delshay and his followers, and that a renegade band of Pinalinos had been allowed to surrender and live at San Carlos in return for these heads.

· · · · · · · · · · · · ·

"Where is Clum? I don't see him at the agency."

"They say he has gone with the soldiers to bring in Geronimo and the Chiricahuas."

"There will be much fighting when the Chiricahua people come here."

This is the way it happened: General Crook had all the soldiers out in the field chasing fewer and fewer Indians. The reservation was the only place where people could build wickiups or make a fire with no fear of the soldiers. Everywhere else the very rocks and hills might hide the bullet that hunted each man who was not where the white man wanted him, which was at San Carlos. So Clum even brought Geronimo there, the shaman riding in a wagon, handcuffs on his wrists and ankles. "This," said Nakaidoklinni, "is how we all should have been brought here. No one should have walked here on his own."

But those Chiricahua stayed there for a winter, taking the rations and resting up, hearing that the land in the mountains they called home, the place that General Howard said would be set aside for the Chiricahua people, was not theirs anymore. And more and more Indians came into San Carlos. It was said that Clum had three thousand, four thousand, five thousand there under his control. Five thousand people who had freely ranged over the wild expanses of Arizona and New Mexico Territory and part of Mexico were herded and fed there at San Carlos.

"They say that the miners have found the white metal on our lands, that they build a town called Globe."

"They say there is a paper from President Grant, taking that land away from us. They say that paper is on the wall at the agency building."

"Someone told me that Clum is leaving, that we get a new agent."

"They say that his name is Hart, that one who will be the agent now."

"There are many fights among the people," said Ilnaba to her husband. "It is not good to have these Warm Springs people, these Chiricahua people, these Yavapai people here with the Tonto and Coyotero and Cibique people. What is there for the young men to do? The people take the corn from the agency and make the *tulapai* to drink. Then they get crazy and fight one another. Then the reservation police come and put them in jail. This is not good, my husband." And the shaman Nakaidoklinni saw these things happen just as Ilnaba said. He saw this suffering of the spirit and took the people's pain into his heart. Sometimes in his dreams he remembered those Tonto people that the soldiers and the scouts had shot. Sometimes he saw the head of Delshay staring with empty eyes. Sometimes he dreamed of Mangas or the dead Cochise and in his dream maybe all these people came together as one. Maybe they saw each other as brothers and sisters of the dark brown skin, people of the black hair. Maybe they said, "What is a Chiricahua? What is a Tonto? Are we not all of White Painted Woman? Did Ussen not put us all here · · · in this place?"

And the name of Nakaidoklinni grew here in San Carlos just as the people swelled in their thousands, just as the pain grew in his heart. For many took sick with the white man diseases and needed their medicine man. Many grew dispirited there in the desert and needed their shaman. The raid, and now even the hunt, was gone. Because the people were given blankets instead of preparing their hides, because they got flour instead of grinding acorns, and because the round of life was the round of the agency, the people took hold of that which was old and familiar, that which could be trusted. And who kept those things now if not the shaman?
· · · · · · · · · · · · ·

The Apache people! A raiding people who subsisted on the land. A people with their myths and religion, their culture and history; a moral people in their own way. Did they have writing? Were their laws in a book? Were their wickiups jails?

Now there was white man law, written in white man books. San Carlos had a jail, where Geronimo was still held. The Apache system of justice was not recognized by the agent or the soldiers. What had been for centuries taken as acceptable punishment was dismissed in a maze of papers, courts, police, and jails, removing from the people the power to police their own society. More than this, who knew what was in the white man books? Who knew when a law might be broken, the police might come, a man taken away—maybe to be hanged, maybe to be sent to the prison at Yuma or Alcatraz?

"They say more metal has been found, that the miners make another town."

"They say that more land has been taken from our reservation for those miners."

"They say the white farmers are taking too much water from the Gila. We do not have enough water for our farms. The corn will not grow without water."

"They say there will be no rations this week. They say the wagons have not come from Tucson."

"These cattle they give us," Sanchez complained, "are all ribs and hooves. Let them give us some cows with meat."

"They say," Ilnaba said on a cold Whiteface day, "the blankets will not come for another moon. The people are cold. The children are cold at night. The old ones feel the cold in their bones and do not sleep at night."

And did a people who never knew money have words for fraud, for graft? Could they see that they were like a cow to be milked, even if they received no hay? Because this is what happened. The agents, the beef contractors, the freight companies, the merchants in Tucson had an Apache cow. It was seen that the agent inspected cattle to be delivered to the reservation, cattle that were big and fat, as the paper said they should be, but then different cattle were driven and delivered to San Carlos. It was seen that the scales at San Carlos on which the cattle were weighed were rigged to weigh hundreds of pounds more than they should to make a fat steer of a skinny one. It was seen that the San Carlos agent arranged to survey the western boundary of the Apache land so that a valuable mine was excluded that he had sold to the son of the Indian commissioner in Washington.

They say the People were known for their cunning,

but the cunning did not run in this direction so highly developed by the white man. The people suffered in their lack of food, shivered in their lack of blankets, and their complaints were heard by those wolves who knew the bleating of the calf, by those who saw there was a cow to be milked if only their halter was ready. So one agent was followed by another, and each one brought his own rope for his new cow.

Still, not all agents were the same. In time, one was appointed who heard the mountain people in their despair ask to go home, and when this simple request was granted, Long Ears took his people back to the valley of the Cibique. His steps were lighter on the way home. It was Nakaidoklinni who was the shaman of the heavy step. It was Nakaidoklinni who carried the tears and cares of the people on his shoulders, who bore them on his back, who took them into his heart, and his step was heavy from the burden of those he sang for, those he cured. And it was heavier for those he sang for who were not cured, for there were many who no longer cared to see the sun rise in the morning.

When the sun rises we cast a pinch of hoddentin toward him,
and we do the same thing to the moon, but not to the stars, saying
"Gun-je-le, chigo-na-ay, si-chi-zi, gun-je-le, inzayu, ijanale,"
meaning "Be good, O Sun, be good." "Dawn, long time let me live."
Words of Mickey Free, from John G. Bourke,
The Medicine Men of the Apache

Back on the Cibique, the spirits of Long Ears' band
began to heal as farms were replanted, wickiups were
rebuilt, and hunters brought in deer. The old ways
once more expressed themselves as the people were
rejuvenated by the land of their fathers. The red cliffs,
the red soil, the old familiar juniper-covered hills,
the green leafy path of the meandering stream; these
were as tonics to the people, just as the barren San
Carlos hills had been a poison.

"I pray I may die in these hills," pleaded Nakaidoklinni. "I pray my bones will contentedly rest in
the earth of this place. I am one with these sunflowers
that grow and flower and seed by this stream. I am
one with the rock that falls from on high, pitching
down the slope to rest until it melts in the wind, until
it washes on down to color these waters. I am one
with the sun. Just as it rises and sets over these hills,
let my life do the same.

"I pray to Ussen, creator of all that is, that my son,
Tulan, will grow to know what it is to be a man. Let

my son see his way through these days so that he will still be an Apache. If the ways of the fathers are not to be the ways of my son, may he find his own way, one that will please the creator. Show him how to live in this land full of white men. I have seen the place where the white men keep the animals in cages. Let my son not be kept in a cage. Let neither the rawhide of the old ways nor chains of the white man bind him.

"I pray for the People. This is a time of trial and great suffering. We have believed that we were placed here to be what we have always been, to do those things we have always done. Our life has been good, and each season we have known what to do, where to go, how to live on this land. We have not wanted in the stomach, we have not wanted in the spirit. Now that has all changed.

"Our old ways have been brought into question as they have been limited by the rules and the power of the white man. But how can we question the old ways when they have been given to us just as the ways of the coyote were given to the coyote people?

"I pray for the survival of all of the People, for all of the Apaches. My nights are haunted by the head of Delshay. I dream of the destruction of the Tonto wickiups, the killing of those bands. I cry for the mountain peoples of the Chiricahuas, for the Warm Springs people who have to leave their hills and go there to the San Carlos.

"When all is against us, we must stand together. I pray that this will happen. We have been people of the band, people of the clan. We have had many chiefs, and each man has stood on his own. This has been the old way for the old times. Now let us stand as one.

"I pray that we have powerful leaders who are wise

and will know what to do. The strong old leaders are gone to the happy place. Give us new leaders to match those of old so that our actions will be full of wisdom.

"I pray that my power keeps strong. I pray that that wolf power stays with me. I have been shown how to cure the pain of the body. I know how to set the broken bone, how to stop a fever. Now the pains I see are not of the bone. I pray to know how to heal the pain of the spirit, how to bring all the people together. It is for these things I listen. It is these things I seek when I fast and meditate as did the old prophets of the white man holy book. I too am a prophet to my people. Visions are given to me of that which may happen to my people. I pray to be given the power to use these visions so that my life will help the People find the new way that Ussen makes for them.

"I see the people choked by revenge, seething with hatred at what has been done to us. Revenge tears at the soul of the Apache, resulting only in more deaths and more sorrows. Let me show how to leave revenge to Ussen so it no longer chokes the chiefs and the warriors.

"I have seen in a vision the yellow cross painted on my medicine shirt. Nasta said the yellow was the yellow of *hoddentin,* the sacred pollen. I need to know the ways of the cross. This is a source of the white man power, and I have seen that that power is great. Let that power come to me, the power of the cross.

"My body is of this land, just as I am of these people. I feel the deep shafts of the miners and the dams of the farmers. I feel the anger of the people. I know of their despair. I know the chill of the bones and the hunger of the stomach. These things I feel; these things I take into myself. I pray for a way to deliver the people of this suffering."

That the medicine man has the faculty of transforming himself into a coyote and other animals at pleasure and then resuming the human form is as implicitly believed in by the American Indians as it was by our own forefathers in Europe.

John G. Bourke,
The Medicine Men of the Apache

It was the *Gan,* long, long ago, who taught the people how to dance. They had harvest dances for when the Earth Is Reddish Brown, just as they had war dances before men left to raid. When those men returned there was another dance celebrating their success and showing off the booty they had captured. In the rounds of the seasons the People danced, their callused feet nudging the earth on its way as they jumped and shuffled and pounded upon its face. When the People danced, everyone became transformed to another time, another place, just as when, in a victory dance, the movements of the warriors celebrating their brave prowess, their bold acts, put everyone there in Mexico where the deeds happened. A good harvest was a call to dance. A bad harvest was a call to dance. People danced when a visiting band showed up, when trading parties arrived, when the rains were late in coming, before a hunt, after its conclusion. Always there was a reason and a need to dance, and each kind of dance had a spirit and form to be followed.

Nakaidoklinni knew the dances of his people, for they had been part of his being ever since he could remember. One learned to dance just as one learned to talk, and both were ways of telling stories, of creating all the little invisible knots that bound a people together into the We of a larger group. But the dance that he started there on the Cibique was a new dance to the People, one that came to Nakaidoklinni much as a power might come in a dream, searching out an unsuspecting but receptive person within whom the power might take root and flourish.

Upon the return from the San Carlos, Nakaidoklinni had resumed his ways of solitary meditation. When he was not being called upon to visit the wickiup of some sick person, the shaman would often be seen climbing up the slopes of the valley, maybe searching out herbs and seeds or bark, but often just looking for the high places where the spirits dwelled. More and more he could feel the presence of the past, the nature of the rocks and trees. He could feel the vibrations from the horny feet of the ancients as they too danced, or had danced, upon the face of the land. Sometimes he followed these vibrations, and maybe he would find himself at the site of some long-forgotten ceremony where the eyes were unable to tell if the past had ever intruded or insinuated itself, where the heart was that which registered the remnants of old sensations and sounds. Nakaidoklinni would pause for a moment or a day, sometimes for four days of fasting and prayer, opening himself to all the forces that wished to be felt, or that he was searching for and desired to feel. Always his bag of *hoddentin* was with him. Always he sought to open his visions to any sign of the white man cross, to any interpretation that could be made of how its power might be secured by the People, of what that power might mean to the future of the Apaches. Each sojourn to the high places was rewarded with new insight, in which the shaman became able to see through the difficulties of the present into a better world that had once been obscured. Because each vision brought more questions, the mountaintops would call again and again, and Nakaidoklinni would once more take up his bag of *hoddentin,* letting the spirits guide his feet to wherever they would take him. Each vision formed a step in a dance that the shaman was learning, each step carrying him on to the next, though no direction was apparent. Yet ground was being covered, questions were being answered, and eventually, over many seasons, it was seen that the steps formed a great wheel, the visions of the future twisting like a hoop back to the present so that now a path appeared to the medicine man where before there had only been high cliffs of sheer rock.

· · · · · · · · · · · · ·

By now Nakaidoklinni was a respected shaman, much sought when sickness prevailed. Many people found their way to his wickiup.

One uncharacteristically gray day he was grinding some herbs and laying in a stock of medicines for the winter when a young man rode up on a large chestnut that was shod with iron shoes and wore a U.S. Army brand. Nakaidoklinni took in the red headband, the military shirt, and the carbine as the man tied his horse and unpacked a haunch of venison. He wore the usual breechcloth over white pants, and when he turned to face Nakaidoklinni a wide ammunition belt with a large U.S. buckle was evident. He looked at Nakaidoklinni a long time before he introduced himself as a member of Pedro's band and a sergeant with the Apache Scouts.

"My boy is sick, so my uncle told me to see if you will help. He doesn't eat or drink, and his skin is hot to the hand."

"How long has that boy of yours been like this?"

"His skin got hot three days ago, and two days ago he quit eating. I ask that you will help him."

As Nakaidoklinni readied to leave, he made preparations for several days. Pedro's camp, on the other side of Camp Apache, was nearly a day's ride. Ilnaba and Tulan would stay behind, so he said good-bye to them, caught his horse, and prepared to ride with the scout who, he had learned, went by the name Dead Shot. As they rode down the Cibique Valley a fine mist began to blow and the sky dimmed further. Both men settled in for a cold, wet journey. It was after dark when at last they rode into a flat full of wickiups, their rounded forms appearing as so many looming mushrooms.

Upon turning the horses loose, Dead Shot led the way to one of the wickiups, from which flickered a pale yellow light. He threw back the flap and invited Nakaidoklinni to enter. A low fire burned, and in its glow were huddled several figures and, on some skins near the fire, a boy of about ten years, who appeared to be asleep. The boy looked drawn, shriveled, and even with his eyes closed, his sockets had a hollow appearance. Nakaidoklinni felt the heat in the boy's face and then the breath, which had ebbed to the point of being barely discernable. Those around the fire said that the boy had been like this since sunup.

On the ride from the Cibique, Nakaidoklinni had listened as Dead Shot spoke first of his son and then of the Apache Scouts and the soldiers at Camp Apache. This boy and his younger brother were the only children that Dead Shot had been able to raise from childhood. Two others had already died, one from smallpox and the other from a fall from a horse. This boy had always been healthy and was big for his age. He was an expert with the bow and was a very good tracker, the one who brought in most of the venison that his mother cooked. When the scouts were out in the field, Dead Shot knew that he could depend on his son. When the scouts were at Camp Apache, Dead Shot and the boy hunted together, and the father taught his son all of the tricks he knew that could be used to track an animal or a man.

Nakaidoklinni looked down on the boy and in his heart felt that this boy's hunting days were over. It was as if a line were drawn on the earth between this world and the world of spirit and the boy was a small hoop to be rolled one way or the other. He was rolling toward the line, wobbling now and then, but rolling faster all the same, and Nakaidoklinni knew that the boy should be removed from the wickiup so his spirit would be free to leave if it wished and the wickiup would not have to be burned. He gave this word to Dead Shot, and the father acted as if he had not heard. Just as Nakaidoklinni was about to repeat himself, Dead Shot stooped to his son, gathered the boy, blankets, and skins, and ducked out of the wickiup.

In front of the wickiup was a large open area used for dances, and it was here that Dead Shot placed his son on the ground, carefully arranging the covers so the boy would be as warm and comfortable as possible. Dry wood was brought up and a burning ember from the wickiup. Quickly a fire was built to further warm the boy: to keep the darkness of night from seeping into his being. Soon long shadows played about the edges of the clearing as those from the wickiup gathered around the still mute form on the ground. Somehow word was being passed to other wickiups. Here and there could be seen a yawning flash as a hide was thrown back from the door of a dwelling, and slowly the small knot of people gathering around the boy and the medicine man was growing.

"What do I do?" thought Nakaidoklinni. This was no case of bear sickness or snake sickness. The boy had not broken a leg or hit his head on a stone. A fire burned within the boy, insidiously smoldering under the skin. The sunken look of the boy's face, the heat that radiated from his forehead told all there was to tell. The shaman knew of no medicine that would help this boy. As this thought expressed itself, a feeling of hopelessness overtook him, a despair that he knew too well. It was the same as the despair he felt about his people. They too were not afflicted with bear sickness or snake sickness, but they were afflicted just the same. Surely the *Gan* knew of something that would help the people and this young boy.

Standing there in his shaman's shirt and medicine hat, Nakaidoklinni contemplated a diagnosis in order to plot a cure. Rattles and roots, dances and chants, amulets and bull roarers, these were the things of the medicine man as he called upon both the powers that he understood and the mysteries of the world beyond. The cure must be a harmonious blend of the powers of earth, man, and spirit, subtly beckoning to the wandering essence of the infirm to settle down and stay a little longer.

"I cannot see through this sickness," the shaman said to himself. Saying this, his hand went to the medicine pouch, closing on the white fur that had led him down the path his life had taken. Closing his eyes, Nakaidoklinni was transformed into a young novice warrior again, keeping watch over his camp, hearing the sounds of the night, the lowing of the cattle. His body was heavy, and a faint but steady thumping drum could be felt, traveling through the earth and up through his feet. There was a chorus of hoary chanting voices from a distant past, accompanied by a far-off howl, long familiar to the medicine man. His body was suspended there in time, each beat of the drum vibrating the sands at his feet, pulling him into the depths.

This was one of those times in his life when Nakaidoklinni was only that which was around him, that which he felt. His mind was quiet, totally absorbed in the essence of the moment, while a greater power showed him scenes from his past, events out of sequence and out of context, seemingly unrelated to each other, yet a thread ran through it all just as beads that had long been sorted by color could just as well be sorted by size or weight or clarity or age. He saw that the events in a life can be arranged according to many schemes, and each has a context of its own: its own special meaning. The set of events that each man chooses to emphasize and collect provides his view of the world, and the shaman saw that some events in his past fit together in ways he had never suspected. Now the time had come for him to allow the pieces to recast themselves and redefine his experience. Opening his eyes, Nakaidoklinni saw that the moon had broken through the darkness, illuminating a patch of cloud and framing a small cross of stars. It was the cross of the fathers in Santa Fe, and its meaning came clear to him. He could feel this new revelation lock into place and knew his world would never be the same again.

The medicine man looked over the gathering as

his consciousness perceived an intense sense of well-being. He made his way in the direction of Dead Shot, who was standing in vigil next to the fire, watching over his son.

"Your boy will be all right now," the shaman predicted. "He will live to hunt again. I know what needs to be done now to cure that boy. These people who are standing here can help, that's for sure! We need them to dance for the spirit of your boy."

Nakaidoklinni arranged the dancers in rays or spokes radiating out from where the boy nestled by the fire. From his pouch of *hoddentin* he took a pinch of the sacred powder and blessed each of the dancers with a purifying sprinkle on the crown and on the breast. Last he blessed the boy and carefully drew on the boy's chest a yellow cross with a ragged outline like the one he had just witnessed in the clouds. The cure could begin.

For four days and four nights the medicine man worked to overcome the struggles for the boy's spirit, the dancers chanting and shuffling as the spokes radiated around the boy, focusing the powers and energy of that place and time to one purpose, one common goal. To Nakaidoklinni, the outcome was never in doubt. The boy would be better, his fever would abate, he would drink and eat again and live to be the man he was meant to be. And in four days, this was so. The boy lived, and Nakaidoklinni made his way back to the Cibique, a new resolve and confidence welling in his breast for the future of the People.

Shortly before Geronimo died he told me that he had never under-
stood why he and Juh could have been influenced to follow the
teachings of Noche-del-klinne. But at that time they were convinced
that the Apaches should leave revenge to Ussen.

Ace Daklugie, son of Juh,
to Eve Ball, in *Troopers West:*
Military and Indian Affairs on the American Frontier,
edited by Ray Brandes

Now the life of the medicine man became a dance.
There on the Cibique, Ilnaba, Tulan, and he built a
big wickiup, much larger than normal, and outside
the main door to the east they made a huge clearing
for dances. When someone sick was brought for a
cure, Nakaidoklinni gathered everyone into the wickiup for a big talk explaining that the spirit of the
People and the spirit of the infirm were entwined,
each affecting the other, and that both must be cured
or the cure would not last.

"Our people are sick because we have lost the way.
Life is not as it once was, and it will never be so again
because these white men have come and drawn lines
on the land. Once everything that we could see was
ours to use and to roam, but it is not so anymore.
Once we went where the fruit was ripe or the deer
were fat. We followed the mescal and the piñon nuts,
and each band had its own favorite places to go when

they felt like it. Each band just went there, and no one told them they couldn't go there. This is why we Apaches make up our own minds about what we are going to do. This is why we don't have any big chiefs who speak for all of the bands.

"Now we can't just go wherever we want anymore. If we do, we get shot at or maybe our women get stolen or our wickiups burned. We can't just get ready and go to win horses in Mexico like we used to. That is in the past. Some say that there will not be a way anymore for a boy to become a man and that all of these things that have changed will make us change too. But, brothers and sisters, I say to you that we are still Apaches and this cannot change.

"We are still the people of White Painted Woman. We are still the people of Child of the Water and of Monster Slayer. We are still the people of this land, and the rocks and trees still speak to us as they always have. What has changed is that now there are these white men. They all dress alike and all speak the same tongue. They all follow the Great White Father and they all listen to their god. They are strong and powerful because they are together and not a bunch of bands acting on their own.

"It is not for the Apaches to become white men. But our old ways are gone, and we must find new ways to be Apaches! I have seen the cities of the white men, and those people are without number. We cannot oppose them with our guns and bows. But let us stand together for what is ours, that which we cannot afford to lose. Let us speak with one voice when one voice is needed. Too often this band or another makes an agreement that all bands are expected to follow. When this happens, let the bands come together for a big talk. Let the chiefs have their say so everyone knows what they think. Then we can decide what to do for all of us.

"Down there at San Carlos we were all pushed together and herded like cattle. Many of the bands fought with each other and couldn't agree on anything. That is how the soldiers got those heads of Delshay. This is what they want, for Apaches to kill each other. But this we must do no more. Let us heal the spirit of the people. Let us not be pushed together like snarling dogs. Let us come together as one. Let us stand for who we are. Let us decide for ourselves what it is going to mean to be an Apache. Let us seek to find our lost Apache spirit and make it strong again. We can do it! Sure we can do it! Then we won't have all these sick people like we have here."

Then the people would move out to the dance ground. Tulan would pour an old iron pot half full with water, cover it with cloth, soap it up to draw it taut, and get the drumstick. Ilnaba would get the *hoddentin,* preparing to shower the dancers in a golden mist. The shaman would minister to the infirm, always applying a cross of *hoddentin,* and then get the dancers set. At first he had to demonstrate the dance because it was traditional for dancers to form as a wheel and not as spokes, but soon the word spread and the people came to know what to expect. It was thus that the people started drawing together, and when the spirit is firm it is easier to hold down the ones who are weak. Nakaidoklinni's reputation as a healer and medicine man spread so that he became the center of a vast wheel, with people coming to him from all points. The spokes in this wheel were many, and they radiated from the big wickiup on the Cibique.

The dance Nakaidoklinni taught the People was a prayer. It beseeched and entreated the gods of the People to heal this Coyotero, to cure this Aravaipa, to remove a curse from this Chiricahua, to invigorate this old Pinalino. Large parties began to make their way to the big wickiup for the ongoing ceremonies, and many people were cured at once through the power of all those people coming together. The shaman received his payment as was the custom, and some thought he was becoming rich, but the horses and cattle that he received and all of the corn and fruit came back to the people who attended the ceremonials, for food was never lacking but freely available for all.

Those who came there to the big wickiup came for a purpose, bringing those with bear sickness: snake sickness, broken arms, burning foreheads, gunshots, aches, pains, and rashes. There was no end to the afflictions that Nakaidoklinni saw. But their purpose brought them together toward a common end, and while they were there, the shaman would talk about the talk that they brought with them.

"We hear that more Mormon farmers are moving near our lands and cutting off the flow of the rivers," someone complained.

Nakaidoklinni had taken to wearing the medal that had been presented to him in Washington. He wore this over his medicine shirt, and it had become part of his shaman's dress. At times like these he would clutch the medal and speak. "I too have heard of these Mormon farmers. They come from the north in their wagons with all their wives and children. They always look for the valleys with water so they can plant their crops and turn their animals loose. They are people of the soil, though not of this soil.

"We cannot use the old ways to deal with these people. We must find new paths, ones that will lead to understanding. We must have water in our streams, for what good is a stream with no water? It is like a body with no heart or a people with no will. No, we must have a will about this. We must stand together. What should we do about these things, my brothers? The lines the white men draw on the land keep us inside these lands and the white men out. But does it keep the waters out too? Let us find a way to stand together in this. What would the wise leaders of old say to us now?"

· · · · · · · · · · · · ·

In this way the shaman was able to make the people think in new ways about new problems for which there were no old solutions. Sometimes he had answers for the people's talk, and other times he discussed the problems in a new way until someone else got the answer. And all the time that this talk and these dances went on, more people came there to the Cibique.

But the people were still Apaches. When they gathered they still made *tulapai,* and some got drunk and then their tongues got loose. Someone would favor taking the dams apart. Someone else would advocate killing the farmers and their families. Then someone would talk about the old days before the white men, and each breast swelled to think that the Apache world could be that way again. All of this was part of the big talk at the big wickiup, and sometimes word filtered back to San Carlos or Camp Apache that the farmers or soldiers or white men would not be allowed to stay.

All the words of the people that they brought with them to the Cibique and all of the words that they made there, the dancing words, the *tulapai* words, the prayer words, Nakaidoklinni took up and worked with in his talks to the people. He tried to let them all work together, just a big pot of words that he kept stirring as the people danced, as Ilnaba sprinkled the *hoddentin* over all in an act of purification, as Tulan and maybe Sanchez beat the drums. And the people kept coming, some from all the bands. Nakaidoklinni saw that they were coalescing, coming together as a people. Some came with passes from San Carlos and some came with no permission at all. Dandy Jim, Skippy, and other scouts came with Dead Shot from Camp Apache and sometimes overstayed the time their officers had given them. Geronimo and Nana and Chihuahua came to the Cibique Valley and set up camps; many of the fighting men of the People were there hearing the medicine man say that new ways must be found with the white man, that bullets and arrows were not enough anymore.

*I have never been able to divest myself of the notion that it would
have been wiser and cheaper to offer this prophet fifty cents a head
for all the ghosts he could resuscitate, and thus expose the absurdity
of his pretensions.*

John G. Bourke,
With General Crook in the Indian Wars

Lieutenant Tom Cruse was the officer in charge of
the twenty-five-man Company A, Apache Scouts. He
reported to General Carr, commander of Camp
Apache, and both served under the department commander, General Willcox, at Fort Whipple.

"Cruse," addressed Carr, "lots of folks are talking
about the dances over at Cibique. Major Tiffany, the
agent at San Carlos, is getting powerful concerned
about what's going on over there. Bands keep going
back and forth without permission. Seems like they
only come back for ration day, and then they're sullen
to boot."

Cruse had known this was coming. Everyone had
heard rumors coming from the Cibique lately. The
day before, the post trader had told him that an
Indian had threatened him after being turned down
for credit. "That's okay," the Apache had muttered,
"pretty soon this will all be ours anyway."

"Yes, sir," Cruse responded, "I agree. I already took
the liberty of sending Sam Bowman over there to

check it out. He should be back in sometime after noon. I've asked Mose and Dead Shot about the doctor over there, but they're mighty tight-mouthed about it."

Cut Mouth Mose was the Apache first sergeant, serving with Sergeants Dead Shot and Dandy Jim and Corporal Skippy. The other members of Company A were young privates, many only two months into their first enlistment. All knew of the shaman from the accounts of Dead Shot, and most had attended some of the dances on the Cibique.

"Several of them rode over there last weekend, and four of them straggled back a day late. Said they had to stay over for a sing for some relative of theirs, but they had been up dancing all weekend and weren't worth much for a couple of days after they got back. They'd had a little too much *tiswin* to drink, if you ask me."

"Well, keep on this, Lieutenant. I want to know what's going on, and I want you to enforce discipline in the scouts. They are in a military outfit, now, Cruse, and I expect you to make that clear to them. Am I making myself clear to you?"

"Yes, sir." Cruse smarted. It was plain that someone had put a burr under the old man's saddle. "I'll bring Bowman in as soon as he gets in, sir."

Sam Bowman was chief of scouts, and Cruse had sent him to Cibique because Bowman was one of a small handful at the camp who spoke Apache. Bowman couldn't read or write, but he picked up the Apache lingo with ease. Cruse thought it was due to Sam being part Choctaw and part black.

Walking out of the commander's office, Cruse glanced toward the small village of wickiups that the scouts had established for themselves. A group of women were standing talking to one another while some boys were playing the hoop-and-pole game out near the parade ground. He noticed that the scouts were gathered in the shade over by the stables.

The shadows were getting long when Bowman rode back into Camp Apache. "General wants to see you right away," informed Cruse.

"Not till I get me something wet. I've been riding hard and it was a scorcher out there."

Carr invited the men in and directed them to have a seat. Bowman's head glistened from a quick dunk in the trough.

"What did you find out there, Sam?" the general began.

"Well, sir, there's a heap of Indians camped out on the Cibique. That doctor's built himself a big wickiup with four doors and he's holding camp meetings just about day and night. These Indians are plenty stirred up about those Mormon farmers and the miners at McMillen, and I can't say I blame them." He looked levelly at the general as he made his report.

"We've heard that that medicine man is telling the people out there that they have got to throw the whites out of the country. Did you hear tell of this?"

Bowman scratched his head and took time in replying, seeming to choose his words. "Well, its like this, General. Those Apaches are going out there 'cause something is bothering them. Now, I ain't saying that they always have a broken leg or anything, if you get my drift. But they all got something they claim is bothering them, that they need to see the doctor about.

"Well, sir, the doctor is might near running without a stop. Every chance he gets he talks to the people in the big wickiup. I can't say that I heard him say that the whites have to be run out. No, I can't exactly say that. But he's telling them that there is a way to keep what's theirs and that they just have to find the way. 'Course, this means different things to different people."

Cruse turned to his chief of scouts. "How is it out there with those Chiricahuas mixed in with the other bands?"

"It's right strange. Those bands are usually at each other's throats, but that ain't so just now. The doctor's got them settled down, that's what he's done." Bowman's face was creased and he scratched his head again. "It ain't normal out there, that's for sure! I got a damned queer feeling about this.

"I've seen this happen before when Indians get to dancing like this, and nothing good's going to come of it. Me, if it's all the same to you, sir, I'm movin' on out of here. I reckon this be my last day at Camp Apache. Time for me to think about going back home."

Carr studied Bowman for some time before answering. He had known Sam for more than two years and knew Sam wasn't yellow. Never before had the general seen Sam get cold feet in a tight situation. "Well, Sam, if that's the way you feel, we got no hold on you. See the paymaster in the morning if you still feel this way." Carr stood up and extended his hand. "You'll be welcome back if you find your way out here again someday."

. . . .

The night was just beginning to cool off, and a light breeze floated up the canyon. On the old lava rim above the Rio Blanco a party of scouts had formed, listening to the river making its way down below.

"Bowman says he's leaving," reported Dead Shot.

Skippy turned. "He told me to stay away from the Cibique. What's he mean, anyway?"

"He thinks the medicine man is going to start some trouble out there."

"He won't start anything. You've heard what he's saying! That is not his way. He knows that won't get us anywhere. He just wants us to find a new way to keep what is ours. What's wrong with that?"

"Maybe Tiffany doesn't want us to keep what is ours." Deadshot had said these words more than once. Everyone knew that Tiffany weighed everything supplied to the reservation twice. He weighed it when he bought it and he weighed it when it was disbursed. But the weights only looked the same when Tiffany used his scales. The Apache had never seen such scraggly beef as they saw since Tiffany had been appointed agent.

"Maybe this is why Bowman is going back where he came from."

*Yes, in the old days I saw war charms, and some had little hoops
of wood on them and some had a little cross of wood on them.
They used them to go to war with and they were holy-respected.*
                    Western Apache Raiding and Warfare:
                    From the Notes of Grenville Goodwin,
                        edited by Keith H. Basso

Nakaidoklinni had a Bible now. He couldn't read it,
but it still lent substance to what he was telling the
people. The medicine man was convinced that the
book and the power of the white man were part of
a whole. The question of how this worked consumed
his thoughts. Daily he thought back to the conversa-
tions of General Howard about the power of the Al-
mighty and how the general said that he had been
sent as an angel to the tribes. The general spoke in
mysterious words and phrases that the shaman had
barely understood. But he had been captivated by
the rapture expressed in the eyes and on the face of
the old man. This he had seen before. He understood
this aspect of the general's dream.

The same feelings had come to him when he talked
with the father in Santa Fe about the resurrection of
the Christ. He knew there was power in that manifesta-
tion of the white man's religion, and the white man
drew on this power in his daily life because in Santa
Fe the cross was to be seen everywhere. It hung from
necks and decorated every wall.

The reality of the resurrection, the link of the once dead Christ with the Father and the life spirit, spoke to Nakaidoklinni. Had he not heard the voices of the dead? Did he not perceive the tie between the power of the spirit and the vigor of the body? So it was that as he made these connections and thought deeply about these matters he naturally took those thoughts to the People. His thoughts turned into wickiup words and went into the pot with all the other words that were mixing and simmering over there on the Cibique.

Some of the People approved of the white man book being used in the dances, but not everyone did. One day, as the medicine man was calling on the spirits of the great leaders to guide the People, Gahcho, a Chiricahua man, stood up and addressed the people.

"Maybe this white man book is good for the Apaches, but maybe it is not. Do we need the white man plow? Do we need the white man wagon? Do we need the white man law?"

A murmur whispered through the crowd as many nodded in agreement with Gahcho. "What we need of the white man," he continued, "is for him to be gone from Apacheria. If the white man book and the white man cross have power for the Apache, let the medicine man use them to resurrect the wise old leaders. I would ask Mangas and Cochise and Victorio what they would have us do."

So did Gahcho spit his words into the pot. It didn't take any extra sticks on the fire to bring them to a roiling boil, and the steam they gave off infused the air there in the big wickiup. And Nakaidoklinni took those words up and worked with them because now these were the meaty words that must be chewed and swallowed.

"This man speaks well. Maybe this book is not good for the people." He paused, and a hush fell over the wickiup.

"In the old days, it was not for us to call back the spirits of the dead. We all know that this was not done. But now Gahcho would hear the words of Cochise. Let us see what Cochise will say of this."

A collective shiver ran through the camps. The people did not like ghosts. When a person died, he was allowed to die outside so his spirit would be free to leave. If death came in the wickiup, it would have to be burned. Even so, some ghosts didn't know where to go or didn't want to leave. When they tried to stay around, sometimes the camp would have to be moved until the ghost became lonely and left for the happy place.

The names of the dead were not called because of fear of their return. Now Gahcho had called aloud the names of the great leaders, and the shaman would try to bring them back to life. Some people left out of fear, but more heard the stories and rode in to see what would come to pass.

· · · · · · · · · · · · · ·

Weary with exhaustion, Nakaidoklinni knew it was a mountaintop night. For too long he had ignored his body and the voice inside as he ministered to his people. Sleep was a precious liquid to immerse oneself in whenever possible, but dancing all night and curing and talking all day left little time for this luxury.

Yet, as much as he needed rest, he needed solitude more. The voice inside and the voices of the land that spoke to him were faint, and he heard them only when his mind was still, when he was at peace.

It was dark when he reached the summit overlooking the camp. A horned moon was close to setting, the starry night brilliantly filling the void above. He stood quietly with eyes closed until he could feel the old ones call to him, and then made his way to a ledge on the far side of the hill. To the rear, a shallow recess in the rock had been walled up sometime long ago, and in front of this, out of the wind, the shaman set up for the night.

Nakaidoklinni felt the weariness ebb from his body as the warmth of the rock flowed up, soaking into his being. The warmth left by the sun infused him with a dark radiance and he gave thanks to Ussen for all life, all things that were.

This night was one of pictures and images that floated through his consciousness. Some he just saw. Others he reached for with his mind and held and turned or brought up close, the better to study them. The voices were quiet, only whispering at odd moments and then in words that were felt rather than heard. The medicine man was infused with the essence of creation.

· · · · · · · · · · · · ·

When the shaman returned to the wickiup the following day, Sanchez and Tulan were waiting for him with four others that Nakaidoklinni recognized as tribal police from San Carlos.

"These man have waited here to speak with you. Tiffany sent them to take you into the agency."

"Oh, our friend the agent wishes to honor me. Tell Major Tiffany that I am pleased to hear of his interest. Tell him I will be able to come see him in one moon. Tell him many sick people need me now or I would come right away. What was it that he wanted of me?"

"He told us to bring you in so that you will stop these dances. Many of these people did not have permission to leave San Carlos."

"It is so that this is not San Carlos," the medicine

man agreed, "but this is still the Apache land agreed to by the Great White Father. Should these people get permission to travel their own lands?"

Another policeman spoke up. "You know our faces, you know our names. You know we have been to these dances, too. Tiffany, he sent us out here, so what are we going to do? We come. Better you come with us than he sends out the soldiers. We will take care of you."

Sanchez reached for his rifle. "We will take care of this man," he taunted. "We don't need any other help. Anyone can see that he is not going anywhere. Tell the major that those are my words and not those of the medicine man. Tell him that you left all your guns back here on the Cibique.

"Tulan, get those guns and then give these men something to eat. They've got a long ride ahead of them back to San Carlos."

When their bodies had emerged from the earth and were visible to their knees they began to sink slowly back. Nana said that he had seen this, and the word of Nana could not be questioned.

Ace Daklugie,
quoted by Eve Ball, in "Cibique: An Apache
Interpretation," from *Troopers West:
Military and Indian Affairs on the American Frontier,*
edited by Ray Brandes

For four days the drums had beat in front of the wickiup. Baskets of *hoddentin* had been sprinkled on all of the swaying dancers as the spokes slowly revolved and then reversed direction. This dance was the ultimate prayer of the People. This dance was the hope that there would be a tomorrow. If there was a time for Ussen to speak, it was now.

Nakaidoklinni knew that he could not perform this ceremony on his own power, as an act of will alone. Instead he had opened himself to the drum, allowing the beat to energize, to provide a sense of order. Ilnaba tried to see that he took food and drink, for in spite of appearance, she knew that he was in a weakened condition. Yet a fervor shone through his eyes, and somehow he carried on.

He knew he was traversing new lands, just like his first raid to Mexico, only now he was the leader. Even though he was still a novice on this trail, he had no question of confidence in his direction, in his decision. He was simply going to see where the trail might lead.

The fourth night, they danced all night watching for the stars that heralded the approaching dawn. All night men took turns standing in the center of the dancers telling stories about the great ones, and everyone had a story to tell from personal experience or one that some clansman had once told around a fire. Each tale had an implied moral of wisdom, strength, or courage.

Near dawn, twelve men accompanied the shaman to the top of the hill above the camp, still dancing to the pulsing drums. A deep chant echoed from Nakaidoklinni as they reached the ridge. The first subtle flush of dawn insinuated itself from the distant horizon as he cried out. "Hear me, my honored brothers. We have danced to remember your days among us. We come here now to counsel with you so we might know how to live, what to do. We call you here as a prayer of the People."

The first rays were like a fog hanging over the vale to the east, like a mist after a gentle rain. Each man's heart beat in unison, silence now pervading all. A rush of wind came to the ears, and each man searched for the sound.

In front of them about thirty paces, the grass and brush rustled as if in a small whirlwind. Each man saw, emerging from the mists, slowly rising with the day and all of the days to come, the forms of the great ones. First the shoulders, then the chests, the waist, the hips. Slowly, three spirits rose from the Earth Mother, their bodies rising until the men could see them to their knees.

Every man who had been there on the hill that morning saw the old ones come back. But not everyone gave the same account of what they said.

It was reported that the shaman talked to Cochise, who said, "Live in peace with the white man."

Nana, who was there on the hill and saw the old ones up to their knees, said they demanded to be left in the world of spirit and stated that the people would have to work out their own troubles.

Sanchez told of Mangas, who promised that the white men would be gone before the corn was ripe.

Gahcho said that he heard that all of the old ones would come back, but only when the white man was driven out.

Perhaps all of the stories told of that morning were so.

The officers, soldiers, the men of the line, the packers and the scouts,
the bull whackers and mule skinners, stage drivers, prospectors and
cowpunchers, the settlers and the Apaches, nearly all who rode
and fought against this great backdrop of Apache Land are gone.
Many died violent deaths and sleep in unmarked graves, yet all
sleep quietly. And the eternal hills remain.

Ross Santee,
Apache Land

The parched deserts of the Rio San Carlos and the forested mountains of the Rio Blanco are very different countries, separated by the sheer cliffs of the Natanes Plateau. When the heaviness of summer rests upon the land and the fruit is growing fast, all the clouds gather over the rim. In the morning a few early risers show up blowing here and there, and then later the rest come on over, congregating in huge billowing masses, towering over everything and extending far above the flight of the mightiest hawk or vulture. There they sit, holding a big talk, using strong words and gathering power until the sparks begin to fly. The sky darkens, and the angry clouds rush off on the heels of the big wind heading toward the mountain peaks of the Rio Blanco or, less often, making a fierce sweeping raid down toward the deserts.

Now there were two storms brewing over the Natanes.

. . . .

Tiffany had a good setup for himself and he planned to keep it that way. He was the only person who knew exactly what supplies were requisitioned for the reservation as well as what was delivered to the bands. If there were shortages here or there, irregularities in the contracts, who was to know?

Supplies came to San Carlos from contractors in Tucson, and they too had their "franchise" on the government, for if you have a cow, you milk her. This loose association of business affiliation came to be known as the Tucson Ring, and it had a definite vested interest in the welfare of the reservation. Particularly, the Tucson Ring's interest was served by peaceful, hungry Indians, because then it was possible to make additional demands on the federal government for additional supplies and fatter contracts.

It was an unsettling experience for Major Tiffany to look out on the parade ground in front of the agency and spy his reservation police riding in without the Cibique doctor. His little gold mine there on the San Carlos was threatened by the rumors and stories emanating from Cibique, some that were now being repeated in Tucson, Globe, and the Mormon settlements. This wasn't the way for an Indian agent to maintain his franchise. His job depended not so much on keeping the Indians happy as on keeping the whites satisfied, their fears at a distance.

"Well, now, ain't you boys something. I send you out to Cibique to bring in one dried-up medicine man, and here you are two days late and empty-handed. And I don't see nary a gun among you. Just which one of you thinks he can tell me where you've been?"

The major looked at each of his men in order and knew from experience that no one was going to volunteer anything.

"What about you, Big Coyote. Where is the doctor?"

Big Coyote turned in his saddle, looking down on the agent. "That medicine man could not come with us 'cause he was doing a big dance, so he is still there on the Cibique. He said to tell you he is sorry he can't come with us. He said he would come to the agency as soon as he can, maybe in one moon."

Tiffany shoved back on the brim of his hat. His eyes were bulging and his complexion was the color of a ripe prickly pear.

"What about you, Red Water." The agent looked at the youngest of his police, a boy from the Aravaipa band. "You all got drunk on *tulapai* and went off and forgot your guns, didn't you?"

All the men looked down at this comment. At last, Red Water replied in a low voice. "Sanchez kept the guns."

Tiffany glared at each man. His little claim there on the San Carlos was being threatened by that skinny, self-styled Apache doctor, and he wasn't about to put up with that. He spat twice on the powdery ground, raising little clouds of dust each time. Then he pulled his hat back down, turned on his heel, and stomped back into the agency office. If his little police force couldn't bring the medicine man in, then he aimed to get General Carr to do the job for him.

· · · · · · · · · · · · ·

Carr had the habit of wiggling his ears when he was deep in thought. His jaw muscles worked in little waves that washed away all the demands of the day so that he could think without interruption.

Captain Hentig and Lieutenant Cruse silently stared in the direction of the commander, their eyes focused just above his head, trying to ignore the flapping ears. When Cruse had first been posted to Camp Apache, he had joked with Hentig about the Old

Man fanning himself with his ears. In the next staff meeting, Carr got particularly worked up and his ears were just a-beating. Hentig tried to keep his gaze out the window, but he heard a choking sound from Cruse's direction and before he thought, he turned to look. Tears were streaming from Cruse's eyes and his face was red from holding his breath. As his eyes met Hentig's, both men burst out laughing. Naturally, they never told Carr what was so funny, but they got the definite idea that the general thought he was the object of their mirth and that he was not amused.

Hentig was aware that Major Tiffany, the San Carlos government man, had directed Carr to remove the doctor who was proving to be such a thorn in the side to the agent. Tiffany, though, was a major only by virtue of his service in the Civil War, and he was outranked by Carr in any event. In fact, Hentig thought, there was no chain of command for Major Tiffany, the civilian, to issue an order to Carr. Other than politics, that is.

Carr, who had been leaning back in his chair, suddenly scraped the legs and sat upright. Reaching into his desk drawer, he fished out a paper and threw it on his desk. Hentig could see that it was a wire addressed to General Carr.

"Here's the nut of the problem, gentlemen. Go ahead and read it, if you want."

Hentig picked up the wire, holding it so that both he and Cruse could read it. It was from General Willcox at Fort Whipple, directing Carr to arrest the medicine man Nakaidoklinni.

"How's that hit you?" Carr asked Hentig.

"I don't see nothing about killing the doctor, like Tiffany wanted."

"I guess there's that," agreed Carr. "If that prophet

would have come in for a talk, like we've asked him to, this would have been a mite easier. Now, with Willcox involved, there ain't much choice, is there? We've got to go out there and pull him out of his tabernacle. I know that Tiffany's behind this, but we're still going to have to arrest the doctor."

"What about the scouts, Cruse? Can we trust them to go along and back us up or should we best leave them here at Apache?"

"I don't like going out there to arrest the doctor in the first place," Cruse said, "with or without the scouts. That's just going to stir things up more, if you ask me."

"That's just it, Cruse. Nobody asked you. All I want to know is if the scouts will be with us or not."

Cruse's eyes bored holes just over the general's head. "I reckon the scouts' record speaks for itself, sir. They have always been a dependable unit in the past. Why should we question them now?"

Carr hated it when he didn't get a straight answer from his young lieutenant. That was not the way West Point had trained him, and he didn't think much of it now. So he kept a tight rein on Cruse, and slowly the young officer was breaking in so that he might amount to something someday.

"All right, Cruse, we will take them with us. Hentig, pass the word that we leave for Cibique early tomorrow. This probably will just be a ride in the country, but I want each man ready for anything that might come up. And we'd better have some extra ammunition along just in case. Are you with us?"

"I'll have the men take their full kit, sir. We'll make sure that it looks like we're prepared for a small war just in case anyone decides to get feisty."

He was a small Indian, physically the least impressive of the twenty-odd Apaches in his "tabernacle." He stood no more than five feet six inches and looked to weigh about a hundred and twenty-five pounds. His face—very light in color for an Apache— was drawn and ascetic-looking. It was an interesting face in every way.

Thomas Cruse,
Apache Days and After

Rich smells of bacon and coffee infused the light breezes beginning to stir over Camp Apache as the sun began building another hot summer day. As the bugler blew stable call, troops D and E of the Sixth Cavalry headed to the adobe corral, each man sizing up his pet troop horse, checking for any signs of lameness, saddle galls, or general poor disposition. The packers brought up five mules to a row of packs and aparejos, threw blinds over the mule eyes, and loaded up, deftly throwing their diamond hitches as they went. One mule carried boxes of ammunition, the others hauled food and equipment.

Orders were passed to mount, and a review formed up on the parade ground. Each man had forage hat, carbine, and slicker. It was the rainy season, and the previous two weeks had brought gully washers every afternoon. As the families of the men watched and waved from the boardwalks around the square, the scouts led the way out of the gate down to the crossing of the Rio Blanco. Here the horses and mules took on a last load of water and the soldiers strung out in single file for the excursion to the Cibique. Soon the men were nearly obscured in a fine cloud of dust, a ghost column freighting out across the countryside, pushed on by the beat of canteens and lariats on saddle leather. Thus they rode as the sun climbed high in the sky till there were no shadows to be seen. Lazy dust devils whirled in the valleys over toward the Rio Negro, shimmering pools of water showing in the distance, never getting any closer.

A halt for the day was called at Carrizo Creek. As the order to dismount was given, the men watered their horses, rolling cigarettes or pulling plugs of tobacco from their troop boots. Strikers went about setting up camp while guards were posted with carbines at the ready. Camp was on a small flat next to the creek. A tight herd of horses and mules was kept on the mesa above. General Carr made sure that his troops looked like a military force ready to do business, knowing that everything his troops did would soon be passed on to the Cibique. Apache eyes were everywhere in this country, and smoke signals could be seen all afternoon.

· · · · · · · · · · · · ·

Everyone there on the Cibique knew the soldiers were coming. They had been expected for days, and now word had come that they had ridden out of Camp Apache. Many of those around Nakaidoklinni urged him to leave and hole up in the mountains until it was safe to come down again.

"If those soldiers come here I will talk with them," he said. "If they say not to hold dances here, then maybe we will move them to San Carlos or near Camp Apache."

"But," worried Ilnaba, "they come because of Tiffany. He wants the dances stopped."

"Of what harm are dances? They help me to take care of our people; they bring us together. Apaches have always danced; we all know this is true. If they come I will talk to them and tell them this. If they take me away, it will not be for long and I will be back here where I belong." But an uneasy feeling pervaded the camp. Many who were gathered there had come without passes. Many were concerned that no harm come to the shaman or that he not be forced to go with the soldiers. But Nakaidoklinni kept these things from his mind, keeping to his duties, tending to those who asked his help; and there was dancing, always dancing.

· · · · · · · · · · · · · ·

From Carrizo Creek the soldiers climbed until they gained the pass where the trail spilled over like a dusty tributary to the well-watered, fertile valley that stretched before their eyes. The hills and slopes were green with the leafy bounty of summer growth. Fields of golden sunflowers flashed in the morning light. Lavender expanses of lupin gently rippled in the breeze. In the distance a low haze of smoke from cook fires was just perceptible.

Lieutenant Cruse stood his horse, rapt in the vision presented before him. It was hard to focus on any particular object, and instead he was absorbed by the panorama. His consciousness drifted and diffused just like the greens and golds before him as his eyes moved to the immense distances where details lost their edges and brightness. They blended and fused into something larger that couldn't be seen, like a tree or a bush or a rock. But he could feel it. It was Apache country that stretched before him, and while he could appreciate the grandeur and be captivated by the expanse, he knew that he was a stranger to the deep rhythms of the land.

Before his posting to Camp Apache he had never considered whether or not he belonged to a given time or place. Home had been home when he was growing up, and even at West Point or in Washington he had never felt like a foreigner. But here he felt like an intruder, an unwelcome guest. He knew that it had to do with his command of the Apache Scouts.

He commanded men who lived in grass huts while he lived in a proper building made of stone and wood and with a roof. That was the real difference between himself and his scouts, but it was an insurmountable difference. A wickiup could be built in a matter of hours from natural materials. A few foraging trips supplied all the food an Apache needed. The wickiup had no permanence; its occupants were not bound to one place. At an owl's hoot it could be burned and the people gone.

In dealing with the scouts, Cruse was always bothered that he could talk to them in broken English but never really know what they thought. What did motivate a man to become a scout? How did they feel about tracking down other Apaches? Cruse could only guess at these answers, and his tenuous suppositions were of no assistance, offered no base from which to answer the question that was really nagging him about the loyalty of the scouts. Always before, the scouts had been dependable. They had served with distinction while bringing in the Tonto Basin bands and in tracking down renegades and outlaws, but Cruse wondered how they felt about leading more than one hundred men out to detain one medicine man whose only crime was holding dances. When he had passed the order to the scouts, Dead Shot had asked why General Carr wanted to arrest the doctor, and there was a surliness in his voice that Cruse had never detected before. He knew that the scouts suspected that Tiffany was behind this Cibique foray, and he wondered what they thought about that.

When it came down to it, Cruse wasn't sure what he thought about this expedition to bring in the doctor. He understood that the unauthorized leaves from San Carlos were an inconvenience to Tiffany, and he knew his sense of military discipline had been disrupted when his scouts returned late from the Cibique camp meeting. But if the doctor wanted to raise all the old dead chiefs from their shadowy graves he was welcome to try, and the sooner the better. These things had a way of running their course, and Cruse thought that nothing would help it along any more than a resurrection failure or two. People only had so much patience with that sort of thing, and he knew the Apaches weren't comfortable in dealing with the dead in the first place.

But orders were orders, and he could sense that the Apaches were stirred up like a rattler that has been poked with a stick. Here these people were driven from their haunts, starved, subjugated, reservationed, and tamed and still whispering that the soldiers would be gone when the corn ripened. Nonsense, but dangerous nonsense.

· · · · · · · · · · · ·

The blue soldiers were coming. The smokes blew their dark warnings, and riders carried word of their progress from the Rio Blanco to the Carrizo, then over the pass into the Cibique. The blue soldiers were coming; a snake winding through the canyons, across the flats, coiling here, testing the winds there, a forked tongue of Apache Scouts, a body of mules, horses, and men leaving a dusty cloud and an echoing rattle of equipment as it slithered past.

And what was Nakaidoklinni to do? Had not every step of his life brought him to this big wickiup? Was he brought there only to run away like a fox or maybe a coyote at the first threatening hiss of a dusty blue snake? These thoughts were in his mind. They were not invited or conjured by him but were there, just like the blue soldiers.

His mind drifted back to his novice days, seeking out those times when the trail had forked and he had stood deciding which way to go. Each fork, each decision had carried him on to the next; they seemed unrelated at first, but were they really? Each fork in the trail of his life had left its marks; there was an experience, a memory, a lesson for each. He could see that they had built upon themselves, providing a movement and a direction for his life. And it had just happened; each decision, made independently of the others, had brought him to this time and this particular place where he had built his wickiup, cared for the sick, and danced for the spirit of his people.

Was there another fork in the trail now, or was there any longer a trail at all? Doesn't every trail carry to a destination and have an end? These thoughts stood in line for his consideration as he went about his day, a day like yesterday, but perhaps not like to-morrow.

"I am a shaman wolf," he thought, "and what more can I be?"

· · · · · · · · · · · · ·

Sanchez watched and waited. His best horse was ready, as were his Winchester and six-shooter. He was naked above the waist and wore just a breechcloth, moccasins, and a cartridge belt. His jet hair flowed long, and he had carefully applied red paint to his body and face. There was a grim set to his jaw, and overall his contenance was one of hard-hearted determination. As Sanchez quietly rode up and down the Cibique, above and below the great wickiup, others joined him or began stripping and making their medicine.

Toward midday, Sergeant Mose and two other scouts rode into the cleared dance ground. Sanchez could see they were nervous and unsure of themselves. Mose walked up to Nakaidoklinni, explaining that the soldiers were coming soon and that General Carr wished to speak with the shaman about the dances.

Nakaidoklinni gazed quietly at Mose for a long time and finally said, "The general knows where to find me. You are welcome to wait." Then he turned and entered the wickiup.

Sanchez sat his horse watching Sergeant Mose. Slowly a group of painted, armed men was assembling in the camp, and the women and children who had heard Mose were traveling back to their wickiups spreading the word. Sanchez knew that the soldiers would have to ride up the canyon until a point where they crossed the Cibique, and it was to this crossing that he now rode and waited.

A shadow is a curious thing. When the sun is overhead in the season of Large Fruit, the shadow is nearly nonexistent. But as the sun rolls on through the sky, the shadows come out, slowly appearing, almost shy. Then with hesitancy, the shadow grows bolder and longer but still not as long as its mate. Slowly, ever so slowly, the shadow grows and blooms, and the more it grows, the faster. Longer and longer it reaches until it overtakes the reality of its opposite, until it exceeds and dominates and conspires with its kind until the shadow world grows and merges, bringing darkness to the world.

As Sanchez sat his horse at the crossing, his shadow began to grow. Initially just a large oval circle on the red earth and grass, then taking on form, a little more substance. It grew a point of an ear, a neck and a nose, a tail. Then long horse legs, a human foot, another, rounder head, and when the shadow had daringly grown to half the size of its opposite, Sanchez could begin to see dust rising down the valley, faint at first, then growing almost like a shadow, but taking on more than just a hard dark edge, more then just a visual quality. Sound was added, a clink here, a tink there, a rolling rock, a murmur of voices. Then Sanchez saw them coming, still in single file, the scouts still leading, and he sat his horse on the trail so the column had to swerve slightly, just breaking around his shadow and then reforming in a straight line while he watched and counted and took inventory of guns, horses, mules, spare ammunition, equipment, absorbing everything as it passed through his shadow and back into the light. And some soldiers gave him hard looks or motioned for him to move back or threw words his way, but Sanchez stood his ground and watched.

When the last horse passed, Sanchez and the men who had joined him closed in, dropped back to avoid the dust, and followed the soldiers up to the big wickiup. All along the way Sanchez noted people streaming out of trees or along the edges of fields, walking and riding, a painted throng converging on the dance ground. Many San Carlos people were also on the path. With satisfaction, Sanchez noted that they also carried their bows and guns with them and were stripped for fighting.

The soldiers formed up on the dance ground surrounded by Apaches, with more up on the slope above the creek. To the right of the big wickiup was an open-sided shelter. Underneath, in its shade, on a pile of Navajo blankets rested Nakaidoklinni. As Sanchez watched General Carr ride up to the arbor with the interpreter, Hurle, he saw that Nakaidoklinni was dressed in his ceremonial clothes, over which he wore the medal presented by the Great White Father in Washington. His garb included the shaman's hat, his medicine cord, and his deerskin shirt. His friend had told him that bullets could not pierce that shirt, and Sanchez wondered if this was why he had chosen to wear it that day.

Carr sat his horse, towering over the shaman. He was not in the mood for preliminaries or niceties but got right to the point. To the interpreter he said, "Say that I have sent him three different messages requesting that he come into Camp Apache and that he has ignored all of them."

With consideration, the shaman replied. "It is true, there have been three messages, but they have not been ignored. There have been many duties to attend to, many people seeking my help. I plan to come as soon as I can."

To this Sanchez knew he might have added that he was also weak from dancing and fasting, but this was left unuttered.

"Tell him," Carr continued, "that many stories have come to white ears from the Cibique and that I must talk of these stories with him. Say that this is why I ordered him to come in to the fort."

As these words were being said, utter silence

reigned around the wickiup. Sanchez could see that more people were streaming into the clearing and that the men were armed and painted. He started to calculate the odds and could see that the soldiers were doing the same, casting measured glances around the clearing. Here and there a rifle was loosened in a scabbard, and several men had their pistols at the ready. As each word was presented, as each thought was completed, the knot of people silently tightened and imperceptibly coiled.

"You are welcome, General Carr, to sit here with me in this shade, and we can talk about whatever is on your mind."

"Tell him," ordered Carr, "that the things that we must discuss will take several days and that he must come with us, now!"

As Hurle repeated these words in Apache, Sanchez felt a coiling quiver assert itself in the tight knot of the People, and an angry hiss rose and then fell as Nakaidoklinni replied.

"There are still a few matters that I must see to here. I will be able to come to Camp Apache in three or four days. There will be time for us to talk then. I cannot go now."

Carr's face stormed scarlet as he heard these words. His left hand tightened on the horn of his saddle and his right moved to his revolver on his hip.

"Tell him," he growled," "that he is coming now and that this is the way it will be. Tell him that if he attempts to evade us that he will be killed instantly. Say that we have charges to discuss with him and that if he is cleared, he can be back in three or four days. Make sure he understands that we are leaving pronto."

At this, a shudder passed through the crowd, and

Sanchez could see it reflected into the soldiers. Many a wary eye was cast about, and the horses began to throw their heads and stamp their feet, sensing the fear and hatred that was enveloping them. A spark was all that was wanted for a fight to ensue, just as the shadows around the big wickiup had lengthened to a parity with their sources. One spark was all that was needed, and every hard heart there was capable of providing it. A rhythmic buzz, an audible warning to back off echoed through the clearing.

Sanchez was tight and hard. There was no thinking about this that was happening. All of these events had a momentum, and they just carried him along, his body reacting, acting on its own. Slowly his knees tightened on his horse, his arm started to raise his Winchester, his focus set on Carr. But just then, Mose and Dead Shot urged their horses between him and Carr, approached the shelter, dismounted, and began to talk to the shaman. In quiet tones that still managed to carry to the crowd, these scouts encouraged Nakai-doklinni to come with them, talking to him but speaking to those gathered around, attempting to defuse, to soothe.

To this Nakaidoklinni replied that he was ready to come and that there was no need to fear his escape. He asked for a short time so his son, Tulan, could bring his horse and so he might gather up a few things. With a slow heave and a sigh, the coiled knot of Apaches released a bit. Carr detailed part of the command to wait and escort the shaman, then he took the rest and moved out, back down the Cibique. Sanchez watched them ride, keeping his eyes on them until they passed round the bend, the general leading them through a cornfield and then out of sight. When Nakaidoklinni was ready, the other troops moved out and Ilnaba was there, walking before her husband, walking backward and easing his way with small golden clouds of *hoddentin*. As they neared the bend, Sanchez saw Nakaidoklinni lead the soldiers across the creek so they would not further trample the corn-fields.

Sanchez noted the shadows now. His own was much longer than he was; the sun rode down onto the ridges that made the valley. He paused there for a time, sitting his horse, casting glances to the multitude gathered there, hearing the buzz of voices, expressions of feeling robbed, a people desecrated, a violation of the Apache spirit. And then he was riding at the front of a group of warriors on the path that led down the Cibique toward the bend around which the soldiers had disappeared.

Below the bend the valley was planted with more fields of corn, well interspersed with tall weeds. To the margins grew vines of squash or melons, yielding to wild grapes. Towering cottonwoods claimed the broad plain where the water coursed, protecting clumps of younger cottonwoods that held together like schools of minnows. The sand was reddish brown, well flecked, running thin to a bar of gravel, deeper in the quiet water. Below this was a shallow rocky crossing, offering sure footing for animals, and above that a small open flat. On this flat General Carr had chosen to make camp for the night. Rounding the bend and clearing the cottonwoods, Sanchez noted that the pack animals were turned out and that the packs and gear had been formed into a circle, in the middle of which stood Nakaidoklinni. The sun just caught him as he turned toward ford. Briefly his eyes met Sanchez's murderous glare, but no flicker of understanding was passed between them. Sanchez was at a loss to know what action the shaman expected or hoped for.

The People had followed Sanchez to the ford, and now some who were walking started to cross on the large flat stones. Some were calling up to the scouts taunting them with names of traitors and cowards. Sanchez could see that the words had their effect, and Dead Shot was plainly arguing with Mose, the other scouts gathered around them.

General Carr pointed down to the ford, yelling to Captain Hentig, who came running down the hill. He was waving his arms, motioning the Indians back across, angrily yelling, "*U-ka-she, u-ka-she.* Get Away." Sanchez and his band were all waving their rifles above their heads, and he saw the scouts drop and load their repeaters. One Apache continued up the hill, ignoring the screaming officer until they closed in a grapple. Seeing this, Sanchez took a deep breath, felt his lungs expand, and then bellowed his battle cry, immediately answered by Dead Shot. Sanchez took aim at Hentig and fired, his the first of a tremendous volley pouring from both sides of the Cibique, and it was a sweet moment for Sanchez because he saw a soldier fall from Dead Shot's bullet, and then all the scouts were also pouring lead into the blue soldiers.

Through the fury and the smoky din, Nakaidoklinni started crawling through the packs and toward the creek. He was just clear of the packs, nearing some brush, when his guard noticed him, raised his rifle, and fired. The shaman collapsed in a heap, then struggled to his knees again just as Sanchez heard an anguished cry from Ilnaba. Once more the blue soldier fired, this time at close range with his pistol, shooting for the head. By now Ilnaba was across the creek and had grabbed the rifle of one of the first soldiers killed. Sanchez watched her as she took ten quick steps toward her husband, raised the rifle to fire at the soldier next to the shaman, and missed. Before she could fire again, she too went down. Next Tulan came up the hill, charging on his pony. He wasn't armed but was going to the assistance of his mother. A storm of lead shot him off his horse. He hit the ground and moved no more.

Sanchez was frozen in time, observing all that was around him. This was a dark day for the People, and he offered a prayer that all of the days to come would not be like this one. But who could see into the seasons and years ahead? It was best, he thought, that the future was obscured, and he wondered how the old ones could have carried on if they could have seen into the days of his life and this day in particular.

He saw that the Apaches were falling back beyond the creek, into the cottonwoods, into the brush up the slopes. The fight had been joined and the fight had been lost. The shaman was dead. He was gathered to the shadows. He now walked in a different world.

AFTERWORD

The battle at Cibique Creek took place on August 30, 1881. The dead included one officer, six enlisted men, six scouts (referred to as deserters), and about eighteen other Apaches. A monument to this battle may still be seen in the small community of Cibique, but nothing exists there to delineate the site of the battle.

A shaman named Nakaidoklinni, sometimes described as a dreamer, doctor, or medicine man, did lead a messianic movement oriented around dances that resulted in the battle. The spelling of his name varies widely in books of Arizona history. (Readers interested in further information about Apache history should consult *The Conquest of Apacheria,* by Dan Thrapp; *Western Apache Raiding and Warfare: From the Notes of Grenville Goodwin,* edited by Keith H. Basso; *Apache Days and After,* by Thomas Cruse; *My Life and Experience among Our Hostile Indians,* by O. O. Howard; and *Apache Chronicle,* by John Upton Terrell.)

Very little is known of the life of Nakaidoklinni. Even estimates of his age at the time he was killed vary greatly. There is no definite photograph of him in existence, but he has been described as being of slight build and light complexion.

The name of the wife of the shaman or of any of his children is lost to history. Ilnaba and Tulan were names chosen for the convenience of this story. The record does show, however, that the wife and son of the shaman were killed at the battle of Cibique.

Certain historical persons from Arizona's past were at Cibique and are also in this book. Examples are General Carr and Sanchez. Although they were real persons, this story is one of fiction, and their thoughts and actions as depicted in this story are creations of the imagination rather than fact.

Of the scouts who sided with their Apache brothers at Cibique, five were arrested and tried for desertion. The record lists their names as Sergeant Dead Shot, Sergeant Dandy Jim, Corporal Skippy, and two privates referred to only as privates 11 and 15. The five scouts were found guilty, the privates serving two years at Alcatraz Island. The other three were sentenced to be hanged, the sentence being carried out on March 3, 1882, at Fort Grant. It is reported that on the day of the hanging, Dead Shot's wife also hanged herself, leaving two young boys.

Of Nakaidoklinni, Lieutenant Cruse and others who described the battle wrote that he was shot a number of times before he was finished off. One report has the coup de grâce being an army hatchet buried in his head. The presidential medal that he wore was taken from his body after the battle and has found its way into the collections of the Arizona Historical Society Museum in Tucson, where it is on display. The motto on the medal is "Let us have peace."